The Christmas MOSAIC

Edited by
Dr. E. White-Elliott

This book contains works of both non-fiction and fiction. In the cases of fictional writings, the stories may have been fashioned after true stories but are not exact retellings.

CLF Publishing, LLC.
9161 Sierra Ave, Ste. 203C
Fontana, CA 92335
www.clfpublishing.org

ISBN # 978-0-9961971-5-1

Printed in the United States of America.

Dedications

This book is dedicated to all aspiring writers who were told they couldn't make it in the field of writing or who may have been too scared to move forward because of the fear of failure.

The thirteen authors, whose stories are included within, are proof that you can be successful and your dreams can be a reality.

So, I invite you to pursue your own writing and be the success you know you are.

C. White-Elliott

Dr. Cassundra White-Elliott

Acknowledgements

I acknowledge all the participants in this project, who helped to see it from its stages of inception to its complete fruition.

May your success be plentiful, as you continue to pursue your educational and writing endeavors. I look forward to working with each of you individually, collectively, or both, in the near future.

Much love and appreciation,

C. White-Elliott

Dr. Cassundra White-Elliott

Table of Contents

The Christmas Monster

J. D. Delgado

"He who fights with monsters might take care, lest he thereby become a monster. And if you gaze for long into the abyss, the abyss also gazes into you."
-Friedrich Nietzsche

It was about a few days before Christmas in the city of Angels, and sixteen-year-old Sarah Nakahara was so excited to celebrate with her family. She had been waiting for months because she made her mother Melissa something very special. Sarah made a crystal heart with the magical powers she was born with. The crystal heart was designed to grant any wish the receiver wanted. However, there were some guidelines. For example, the holder could not make a wish while feeling anger or jealousy. The reason behind that is because the emotions of anger and jealousy are the kind of emotions that we feel in the moment. Only the holder could make any wish he or she wanted, unless he or she allowed someone else to make a wish.

Elsewhere, Katie Madison was a sixteen year old who hated Christmas. She hated everything it stood for. She hated good people and people who were happy. All she wanted was to see everyone in misery. Like Sarah, she also had powers. But, she used them for evil. She always terrorized passerby's by reading their minds and playing their worst fears in their minds. She was a very tortured soul. She lived all alone on Mount Golgotha, also known as the place of the skull. The only one she could never scare was Sarah because of the fact that she also had powers.

Both of the girls had one thing in common however. When they felt extreme emotion, they become huge wolves. Sarah was a white wolf because she had a pure heart. Her eyes shined a brilliant crystal clear blue. Her eyes were very hypnotizing at first glance. Katie was a black wolf because she was so evil that it reflected off her wolf persona. Her fur was darker than night itself. Her eyes shined a burning red like embers from a slowly dying fire.

One day, Sarah was on her way to school. She smiled, waved, and said hello to everyone she passed by on the street. While she was walking, her eyes met with Katie's. The two girls had no idea what to do. Sarah, who was normally the extrovert and happy, was suddenly stopped in her tracks. She was curious and afraid of Katie at the same time. Just like Sarah, Katie was also getting the exact opposite reaction of how she normally acted. Katie's mind filled up with happy thoughts, and she almost cracked a smile. After the strange encounter of mixed up topsy-turvy emotions, the two just awkwardly walked away, but basically they went in the same direction because they both went to Aurora Wilson High School.

Sarah went to her friends Savannah Luna and Jenny Dean to talk about how they were going to plan their ultimate Christmas party. Savannah suggested they have the party at her house. Jenny said, "There's no way we can fit more than ten people in that house, and if we've forgotten, Sarah is claustrophobic." Savannah realized her mistake and slumped her head down. Savannah then looked up at Sarah and asked, "So, where do you want to have the party, Sarah?" Sarah then suggested that the trio host their party at her house since it was a huge mansion. The place could fit over one thousand people and still have a lot of extra space left over, whichever way you turned whether it was inside or outside. All was settled; the Christmas party of the millennium was on!

Katie was at school listening to the whole thing. She was secretly hoping that she would get an invitation. Nothing had been going right for her lately. Her mother kept pushing her to graduate from high school, but she was failing. She was working long unusual hours for a teen her age. She didn't have a friend or significant other. She felt alone in the world. She wished someone would pay attention to her, but that wasn't happening any time soon. Instead, Katie wanted to devise a plan that would sabotage the party. She would need her old Halloween decorations because she wanted the Christmas party to be one made from hell.

Sarah took Jenny and Savannah shopping for the party after their sixth period was over. They headed over to Festivities Central in downtown City of Angels. Festivities Central was the place to go if you needed some out-of-this-world party favors or ideas for any occasion. The trio bought balloons, plates, plastic utensils, streamers, banners, a giant train set, and many other supplies needed for decorations.

Meanwhile, Katie was contemplating how she would crash the party. She thought of old scary Halloween tricks, pranks, and monsters she could use in order to scare the living nightmares out of the party guests. She was having second thoughts though because she actually took a liking to Sarah. She felt bad, but at the same time she just wanted to get attention.

The day of the party arrived and more than half of the town showed up. There were twenty-five foot Christmas trees put up and decorated with colorful lights and ornaments with pictures of people from the town. Mariah Carey was a special guest at the party because Sarah was her cousin, and her favorite Christmas song was "All I Want for Christmas Is You." Everything was going great until the lights went out. Strobe lights started flashing all around the party. Scary noises were playing, and hologram monsters were being projected and scaring the guests!

Sarah's eyes started glowing blue with her anger rising inside her. Someone was trying to ruin her party. Off in the distance, Sarah spotted a black wolf running. She then knew who ruined the party. It was Katie. Sarah started changing into her white wolf form and chased Katie down. It started snowing, but wolf-Sarah caught up to wolf-Katie and tackled her down. The two fought with fangs and claws until finally both just collapsed in the snow.

Katie now back as a girl began to apologize to Sarah. She explained that she was very sorry and didn't know what she was thinking. That's when Katie broke the news. They were long lost sisters who were abandoned in the forest when they were younger. The real reason why they were so different was because they were both adopted by wolves of rival packs.

The two finally realized that they had really abnormal lives, but that it was time to move on and live in the present. The two enemies reconciled and lived as sisters in Sarah's mansion.

About the Author

J. D. Delgado is an author that loves writing stories that tickle the minds of readers. He was born in Orange, CA but spent most of his life in Anaheim and Fullerton. He grew up as an only child with a single mother trying to make ends meet. J. D., as a child, was a great writer and speller. It wasn't until recently in 2015 that he decided that he had unfinished business. He began writing again for the sake of readers who were hungry to read more stories that have not been told yet.

Edited by Dr. C. White-Elliott

The Gift of Giving

Shawna Festa

"It is Christmas every time you let God love others through you...yes, it is Christmas every time you smile at your brother and offer him your hand."
-Mother Teresa

Jane started her day like any other. Her alarm sounded off much too soon and could be heard throughout her small, South Hampton home. Through her window, she could see the fresh snowfall from the previous night. Immediately, she was reminded Christmas was only just two weeks away. Since her husband's death a few years back, Jane still had a hard time coming to grips with the holidays. With three young children still at home, it was still the hardest part of the year. Jane's husband was killed in a fatal crash, only two months before Christmas. Although it had been three years since the accident, sometimes it felt only like yesterday. Every Christmas, birthday, anniversary and holiday, Jane was reminded of that horrific day. As much as life might be at a standstill for Jane, she knew she had to be strong and continue on for her children. Marie, a very eccentric five year old, was the youngest; Joey, her only son, was seven; and Annie, her oldest daughter, had just turned nine.

As Jane went about her usual routine, she thought about Christmas and what she would get the children as gifts. That was the hardest part about the holiday. Placing senseless gifts under the tree for the children to enjoy, knowing the one thing they wanted that she couldn't give them, broke her heart. Daddy was not coming back home. Jane shook her morning thoughts away when Marie came and jumped on the bed.

"Mommy, can you make pancakes for us? The ones with blueberries? Pleeeeaassseee."

"Mom, Annie is hogging up the bathroom and won't get out! Tell her to get out. I have to go to the bathroom," Joey complained. Jane scooped up the bouncing kindergartener in one swift scoop as she crawled out of bed.

"No pancakes today. Mommy is in a hurry. Let's go get dressed for school. Annie, let your brother use the bathroom."

After getting ready for school and dressing Marie, Jane went to the kitchen to prepare breakfast. Cereal. That was the gist of weekday breakfast in the Peterson household. The front door flew open as Barbara, Jane's mother-in-law walked through.

"Grandma!!" Annie yelled as she went to give Barbara a big hug.

"Good morning, my sweet princess! Grandma brought you a treat!"

"Doughnuts are hardly adequate for breakfast!" Jane exclaimed.

"Nonsense! It's breakfast of the champions! Besides, it's not any worse than the junk in that cereal box you're going to feed them," Barbara replied.

"Yaaaa, doughnuts!" Marie screeched. Jane shook her head in disapproval as she headed to the back room. She had already lost the battle. However, she couldn't complain.

Barbara had been a tremendous help since Michael's death. In fact, Jane didn't know what she would do without her most of the time. Barbara came by every morning to get the kids off to school and again to pick them up from school in the afternoon while Jane went to work. Jane was a police officer in the north subdivision. She loved her job, mostly. Sadly, the holidays were the busiest time for her law enforcement career. People desperately seeking gifts for their families resulted in theft, accidents, and even worse, robberies. People were scurrying around to get the perfect gift for their loved ones. It seemed like everyone around was in a panicked rush.

As Jane's world was at a standstill from Michael's death, she could see it more clearly. Michael hated Christmas. No, not the true meaning of Christmas, but the commercial aspects that were tied to it. People buying senseless gifts just to have something to wrap and put under the tree. He hated that people didn't understand the meaning behind the holiday or gifts. Michael was a giver with a tender heart for all. He was a detective for the same police department where they met fourteen years before. Countless times, he would purchase items for the homeless or children who went without, from a pair of shoes to a doll for the little girl who was placed into foster care because her parents were arrested and in jail. None of it went to waste for him. Jane would tell him, "You can't save everyone." Although Michael knew he couldn't save the world and everyone in need, it never stopped him from giving what he could. Jane missed that about him.

Jane's day was much like all the others. She drove past bell ringers, beggars, and responded to a heated domestic violence call. There was nothing really out of the ordinary, until she got the call of a nine-year-old girl caught shoplifting. As Jane walked up to the store, she was caught off guard to see the little girl, being detained in a chair. Her hair ratted, shoes with the soles coming apart, and no jacket despite the freezing weather outside. The little girl looked up with sad eyes. Next to her was the store manager, holding a boy's jacket and mittens.

"Thank God, you are here! This little rat was stealing from my store! She tried to walk out wearing a jacket, mittens and large silk sweatshirt! This is $258 worth of merchandise, and I want her taken away! Children these days have no decency!"

"I will take it from here. Thank you," replied Jane, as she took a seat next to the little girl. "What's your name?" Jane asked her. She didn't respond. Jane noticed the jacket and mittens she was stealing were much too small for her, and the jacket was a boy's winter coat. She also noticed the silk sweatshirt was much too large for her to fit.

"I think I can see what is going on here," Jane told the little girl in a soft voice, "but I can't help you if you don't talk to me." The little girl looked up at Jane with sad eyes.

"My name is Annabelle. I'm really sorry I took these things. I know it's wrong to take things that don't belong to me, and I'm sorry."

"Are these things for you?" asked Jane.

"No. The jacket and mittens are for my little brother. He is six. Mom says he can't play outside at school on days it is cold outside because he will get sick. He wants to play outside, and he needs a jacket and hand warmers because he doesn't have any," Anabelle replied.

"And who is the sweatshirt for?" Jane asked. Annabel's eyes lit up.

"That is for my mama," Annabel replied.

"You know, Annabel, it is against the law to steal. People get into big, big trouble for stealing," Jane said. Annabelle looked down sadly.

"I know it is wrong to steal. I just really, really wanted to help. I asked Santa for money for Christmas, so I could bring the money back to the store and pay for it. I swear." She pulled a folded up note from her pocket and handed the note to Jane that read:

Dear Santa,

In my last letter, I asked for a superstar Barbie. Instead can I please have $100 instead, so I can buy my brother a jacket? Thank you, Santa for everything. I will bake your favorite cookies for Christmas Eve.

Jane's eyes teared up. She stood up and escorted Annabel out of the store, leaving the manager with a lost expression on his face. Jane took Annabel home. As she pulled up to the rickety home on the south end of town, Annabel's mother ran out to greet them.

"I am sorry. This will never happen again! Annabel, get in the house. What were you thinking? You know better. I have never been so disappointed in my entire life!" Jane felt bad for the family as they walked away. The little girl was so desperate to get the things her family needed. Maybe not just for Christmas, but in general. As Jane clocked out from her shift that night, she had a heavy heart. She drove home and thought about her own children and what Michael would have done. She knew what Michael would have done.

Jane walked in the door at home just in time for dinner. Barbara made her specialty, baked spaghetti, and it smelled delicious. "Mommy is home, yippy," Marie rushed to the door to greet her as she always did. Jane forgot about the details of her shift and was happy to be home. Joey and Anne were discussing the details of their day. Joey got an A on his math quiz and was thrilled. Anne talked about a girl who sat next to her, and she got to share her pencils with her because she never has one.

"Bobby says Santa isn't real. He laughed at me, and the other kids laughed at me too."

"Nonsense!" Barbara replied.

"Mommy, we played duck-duck-goose today, and I won," Marie said.

"No one wins duck-duck-goose, silly," chimed Joey.

As dinner came to an end, Jane was thankful for her children and for Barbara. She felt beyond blessed to have them in her life. She just wished Michael were still a part of it all. She missed him so much sometimes she couldn't bare it. Oh, how her children did bring her so much joy, but since the accident something huge was missing for them all. And they all felt it every day. Jane wished she could be as resilient as a young child. Even where there is loss, children seem to never lose their vitality.

The following day was Saturday. Jane had the day off work, and the children were going with their Uncle Bobby to go ice skating. Bobby was Michael's younger brother and enjoyed taking the kids out from time to time. She planned the day for Christmas shopping. All of her children still believed in Santa Claus, which Jane struggled with. Jane wished she could think of a way to remove the focus of Santa Claus and replace it with something more meaningful. Perhaps as they grew older she would think of something.

As Jane left her house the following morning, she had a list of items her kids wished for. Jane hated buying useless gifts. Trying to keep up with the Santa Claus persona seemed empty to her now, but she wanted to keep the magic of Christmas alive for her children. As she scanned the store for the perfect items to match her wish list, she came across the little boy's jacket from the previous day, the one Annabel tried taking for her little brother. Jane stood still for a moment as she remembered the sadness she saw in the little girl's eyes. She placed the jacket in her cart and continued on to the shoes and sparkly sweatshirt the girl also wanted. And as she went through the toy aisle, she placed the superstar Barbie in her cart as well. Eventually, Jane had a cart full of items for the girl and her family. She was overcome with a sense of zeal she hadn't felt in a long time.

As she stood in line to check out, she looked over the items in her shopping cart with joy. "Ma'am, I can help you over here," a man's voice declared. It was the angry store manager from the day before. As Jane began unloading her items from the cart, he greeted her with a welcome smile, and she could tell he recognized her from the day before. "Day off work today, huh?" He didn't mention anything about the young girl caught shoplifting. As he scanned the items, he stared at the jacket, mittens and sweatshirt. He looked up at Jane with a shocked expression.

"Ma'am, if you don't mind my intrusion, are these items for the little girl from yesterday?"

Jane, shyly and slightly embarrassed, nodded her head. "Yes, please don't judge too harshly," she laughed.

"Not judging at all. I couldn't stop thinking about it my whole shift yesterday. In my twenty years of working retail, I've never experienced what I witnessed yesterday. I went home wishing I would have done something myself. Please let me donate these items," the store manager offered in reply.

"No, no, that's not necessary, but thank you," Jane said.

He insisted with a heartfelt stare, "Please, give me the gift of giving today. It will give me more joy than you know."

"Of course," Jane smiled. "The family will be most thankful."

Jane left the store feeling a sense of great joy she hadn't felt in a long while. She had an idea. She wanted to pass the feeling she was feeling on to her children. When Jane got home, the children had already returned from their afternoon out with their uncle Bobby. She thanked Bobby for taking the children out for the afternoon. "Anne, Marie, and Joey, get your coats on. We are going out," Jane told the kids. "We are going shopping." Excitedly, the three children loaded up in the car. "I want a new Barbie," said Marie. "I'm getting a new Ninja Turtle face mask, and I'm going to be Michelangelo," Joey said. "I want the new Descendant's movie!" Anne replied.

As the excited carload pulled up to the store, Jane shut off the car. She turned to the three excited faces sitting in the back. She handed each of them a $20 bill. The children looked up to her with confusion.

"I am giving each of you $20 to buy a gift... for someone else. Not just any gift. I want you to find something someone needs. I will be waiting in the coffee shop at the front of the store. When you are finished, come back and show me what you bought."

The children rushed into the store with excitement. An hour later, Jane started to look around, slightly worried, just as Anne, Marie and Joey were making their way out. They were chatting happily as they made their way back to the car. On the car ride home, the children discussed the special items they had chosen.

Anne bought a pencil box for a little girl in school who never had her own. It was pink and sparkly, full of pencils, erasers, and even glitter pens. Anne was sure her classmate would be thrilled. Joey bought a backpack for a kid at school who didn't have one. Marie bought a teddy bear for a girl at school who played alone because she never had a toy to share at 'show and tell.' As the children discussed their items, Jane could hear the joy that replaced the excitement they initially had. She was glad they all understood the concept of what she wanted, and they all purchased necessary items. When they arrived back home, they were anxious to wrap their gifts to take to school the coming Monday.

As the weekend flew by, the kids were mostly excited about the last day of school. Not because it would be Christmas break, but because of the unexpected gifts they had to give away. Marie said the little girl cried when she received her new teddy bear and asked Marie to be her friend.

The days flew by, and before long, it was Christmas Eve. Jane beautifully wrapped a few items in bright, shiny red paper, and wrapped them with beautiful bows. She then placed them under the tree and called Anne, Joey and Marie to sit. Jane explained these gifts were for a family she met, and that we were going to deliver them. "Tonight, we are going to deliver these items to this family. Not because they have asked for them, or because they want them, but because they need them. Your father used to tell me, 'The best gift of all lies in the gift of giving.' And that is what we are doing."

They pulled up to the rickety home Jane had visited just a week before. The woman immediately came outside, slightly confused, with Annabel by her side.

"Hi, Annabel," said Anne. Surprised Anne knew who she was, Jane asked, "Anne, you know Annabel?"

"Yes, we are in the same class. That's who I got my gift for," Anne replied with a shy smile.

Jane explained to Annabel's mother why they were there. "Please allow us the gift of giving. Since my husband passed away just a few years back, there is nothing that would give us as much joy." The woman, Meredith, invited them in. They all chatted for a long while. Meredith had lost her husband just a few years back too. Since then, she just hadn't been able to keep up with the spirit of Christmas.

The two women chatted over coffee and had much more in common than Jane thought. They both despised the frantic and commercial aspects of Christmas. The children all became acquainted. Anne and Anabelle became friends. On the way home, Marie said, "Mommy, I feel like Daddy is here with us today."

"Me, too," said Joey. Jane agreed. For the first time in three years, she felt the fulfillment of Christmas.

The Peterson family looked forward to the shiny, red wrapped presents under the tree every year. It became a tradition, and they all felt Daddy was still with them. Maybe not in person, but in spirit, the spirit of Christmas.

When presents are not gifts, they are just presents. Most times there is no true meaning behind them. People rush around, in the hustle and bustle of what Christmas has become, fulfilling items they think others want, but rarely what one truly needs. It can be a coat, a backpack, a pair of shoes or even a scarf. The most special gift of all is a gift associated with an emotion, such as gratitude, happiness, generosity, joy, and love.

This year, look within yourself and find how you can bring the spirit back into Christmas, with the gifts of giving and not just presents. Giving what truly matters is where you will find the gift of giving.

About the Author

Shawna Festa has always had an excitement for life, always looking for the next chapter. Since a young girl, she has always had a special interest in reading and writing. "It takes me away to another place, where I can enjoy different chapters of someone else's story," she says. Shawna is thirty-three years old, a mother of two living in Yucaipa, CA. Currently a professional hair dresser, Shawna is currently pursuing a career in education. "I want to touch people on a different level- people like me, people who need to see things a different way," she says.

The Ornament Contains

Mireya Garcia

"Life isn't about finding yourself.
Life is about creating yourself."
-George Bernard Shaw

Alone he stands at the bus stop. The time schedule reads the bus would arrive approximately at 8:40pm. Checking the watch on his wrist, the time is 8:34pm. Smiling to meet an old memory. Every night that contains this similar plan, the heart gets broken. Change. Change is a must this time. His siblings and their family would be expecting him to return by midnight. There's a smile to trick himself into believing there will be change.

She hastily walks towards the bus stop. The bus can take her to a new area unknown to her. Her mind is playing a loop of recent memory. If she cries, then she'll lose her mental battle of trying to forget. Fast movement is helping. If she slows down, the loop will repeat quicker. She sits down.

She is next to him. He's observing her with his peripheral vision. She's jittery and adjusts her sitting position as if there's a chance she'll feel cushions of a couch. When she's not adjusting, she's looking at the concrete before her feet, while tapping her heel quickly and silently.

There's no harm in distracting himself. She would be more relaxed by having a conversation. Connecting with one another is a medication. However, convincing another to have a conversation is an art that needs to be performed.

"So. Where you heading?" he asks.

"I don't know. I'm just going. I guess," she replies.

Her voice sounds as though she's running away. Those words translated to she had no plans. The last thing she needed was to be alone. Who knows what type of actions she might do? She needs a friend. A chaperone.

"What scared you off?" he asks.

"What do you mean? I'm not scared."

"Oh. Well. I only meant what brought you here? To the bus stop."

"My stupid boyfriend."

"He did something stupid?" He slightly laughs.

"Yes. He doesn't care and feels as if he can do what he wants."

"What did he do?"

"He broke my mother's ornament, and he's behaving as if it's no big deal. He didn't even say sorry. After the whole thing, I just stormed off."

"What significance did the ornament have?"

"The ornament has a lot of Christmas memories...and my mother died a few years ago."

Tears start to stream. To prevent from crying, she starts to breathe through her nose, while fanning her hands towards her eyes to dry the stream.

"I see. You still want to behave as if she's still here. Come with me. You don't know where you're going, but I know where I am. Tag along."

The bus slowly stops in front of them. He stands up and puts his hand towards her as a gentleman. The hand looks as if nothing bad is going to happen. It is so inviting. After she accepts, he helps her up. The bus is not filled. Most people are with their families already. Of all the seats, the nearest seats are a pleasant image for sitting.

"Are we heading to your family?" she asks.

"No. I'll go to them after."

"Where are we going?"

"Let's leave it as a surprise. Think of it as a Christmas present, but you can open it early."

His short answers keep her mind still. The silence fills her with thoughts of her boyfriend, the ornament, and her mother. The significance of the ornament, her only connection to her mother is now gone.

"So, why are you on the bus?" she asks.

"The present. Don't rush. How did your boyfriend break the ornament?"

"Let's just enjoy the silence then." She smiles.

When she had walked in, her boyfriend was decorating his Christmas tree. To make the tree represent both of them, she had brought her ornaments. She set her box to the side and hugged him with Christmas in mind. It would be their first Christmas together. The sun had gone down, and he gave the news of finishing the tree, while she was still in the process of making lasagna. She smiled. But the image of the tree removed the light from her face.

She asked about her ornaments. He attempted to persuade her with the excuse that his ornaments needed the whole tree and to replace a few of them would've been ridiculous. They strained their voices. Eventually picking up her mother's ornament, she exclaimed the vivid beauty of the surface and the inside contained memories. He then smacked the ornament out of her hands to release the trapped memories.

"After we go, I'll be going back to my older sister's house. My family is there. They're fun to be with and are very comforting for me."

"Spending time with loved ones should be fun, especially at Christmas. That's what Christmas is about," she says while looking at the ground, projecting her thoughts. He smiles to remove the darkness on his face before she was able to look up.

"Stand up with me. We're about to get off and walk a block."

They both walk off the bus. He leads her to the entrance which was her present. The entrance is a gate. There is darkness behind those gates. Walls to keep the darkness contained inside.

"He who enters leave hope here," he humorously says, trying to spark a bit of light. "Not sure if that's the true quote though."

"The cemetery?" she asks.

"But of course."

"Why would you come here?" Her heart starts racing in confusion. The question distracts her mind.

"Don't get scared. There's cameras here, so we'll be safe by the security guards."

"That's only if they're looking," she says.

"You make a point. C'mon, let's jump the wall."

"What? I thought you said there were cameras?"

"As long as we're not stealing, security should be fine with it. They know people grieve."

They jump over the wall and walk for a few moments. Her arms cover her body, trying to feel safe, while expecting spooks. His arms are down, and his back is straight. He is very casual. *He's done this before,* she thinks. Their steps become shorter distances until they aren't steps anymore. He turns around to face her and moves his hand to tell her eyes where to go.

"Here we are."

"Oh. Who is this?"

"This is my wife. Or at least the memory of her. It's been five years now. I visit every Christmas Eve, but I don't like to."

"Then why do you come?"

"She believed that Christmas is meant to be spent with loved ones. That's not my eye on the case. Christmas is about having fun and enjoyment; it doesn't matter whom you're with. Love, hate, neutral, or anonymous. It's hard for me to have fun on Christmas. Christmas is just plastered with her. I don't want to remember her, but... I still come."

"I see."

"Time is fragile, and it's slowly breaking every moment. Since it's breaking, you should let it break for good reasons. That's all I wanted to show you. I've held that thought for three years now. Unfortunately for me, these walls are my cage, not hers." He gives another smile.

"Thanks."

"Now that I've shown my gift to you. You can continue running. Run in any direction or stay still. Nice meeting you. Goodbye."

Back on the bus, she stares at the floor, above her feet. Heels are not tapping. The floor has the image of his smile. The vivid beauty of the smile that contains dark memories inside. Those memories with walls that he jumps over. The stranger's smile.

She returns to the entrance containing her boyfriend. His quote rings in her mind.

"Stacy! Where'd you go?"

"The cemetery."

"Why there?"

"I don't know. But, I came back. And, I came back to break up with you."

"What?"

"What's the point of Christmas for me, if I'm not going to have a good time being with you?"

"Because we love each other. That's the point. It's the time to love and appreciate that we have each other. Appreciate the times we had. Our memories of each other. Like when we ate pizza and laid down staring at the stars while talking. I love you."

"Then, why couldn't my ornaments be on your tree? Why only yours?" The lungs finally had time to relax and catch clean air. "No. I'm sorry, but we're done."

"You don't love me?"

"Not the point because I do. I'm just able to enjoy Christmas alone or with my other friends. I think that's what I'll do. Have a good Christmas. Goodbye."

The door between them now kept him inside just like the darkness in the cemetery. She boards the bus once again. The floor, again, has the stranger's smile. Shortly after, she departs the bus and appears at a door. Before knocking, she leaves hope and pretends. She adopts the smile of the stranger. The door opens.

"Hey, Gina."

"Hey, Stacy. Where's Brad?"

"He's at his place."

"Oh. Come in. Hopefully, you'll have fun."

"Don't worry. I know I will."

About the Author

Mireya Garcia Diaz is Hispanic and was born in Indio, CA on November 21, 1996. She is eighteen years old. She grew up in a lot of places, but Los Angeles happens to be the most memorable for her. She moved back to Indio when she was around nine years old. She is the youngest in her family with three older siblings: two brothers and one sister. She has three nephews and two nieces. She graduated from Shadow Hills High School on May 30, 2015. She loves adventures and enjoys music very much. She is currently learning how to play the piano. She also loves to sing but is very shy to sing in front of people. She is artsy, liking ceramics, drawing, painting, and sewing. She is a creative person and thanks her mother for that because she is also extremely creative. Every day is a blessing, and she is super grateful for everything in her life.

Edited by Dr. C. White-Elliott

A Home

for Christmas

Misty Hamby

"The greatest contribution to the Kingdom of God may not be something you do but someone you raise."
– Andy Stanley

In the early 1980's, an eight-year-old boy named Malakai lived in an orphanage in Los Angeles, California, along with several other children. An orphan meant being unloved and unwanted in the eyes of Malakai. Every day of the year, the orphans spent their days working from sunrise to sunset. They worked in fields, cooked and cleaned and did their own laundry. The orphans were hardly fed and were told to be grateful for what they were given. Malakai could not recall a time he was ever able to call anything his own. He always dreamt of having a family of his own.

Once a month, families would come and visit the orphanage to meet and interact with the orphans. On those days, some of the orphans would find their forever homes. But for Malakai, those days were just another reminder that he was unloved and unwanted. Malakai had been in the orphanage for five years. He was beginning to think he was never to be adopted.

It was late December. All the trees were barren, the weather was cooler, and Christmas was just a few days away. It was time for the families to come to visit. That time, they all came with baskets full of sweets: red and green frosted cupcakes and sugar cookies cut into Christmas trees and white and red candy canes, which were Malakai's favorite.

A new family came that day, one Malakai had never seen before. He especially noticed a beautiful woman. Her hair fell to her shoulders and seemed to be spun of pure gold, just like he read in his story of Goldilocks. Her smile was radiant and brightened up the whole room. She had enchanting big brown eyes. She walked with her arm linked with a tall broad-shouldered man. He also looked warm and welcoming to Malakai. *They are perfect,* Malakai thought to himself.

They started to walk towards Malakai. "Hello, my name is Patricia, and this is my husband Timothy. What is your name?" Malakai was so nervous, but somehow he felt so connected with them. Instead of answering her question, Malakai felt compelled to launch himself into the woman's arms and give her a hug instead of his name.

The director of the orphanage seeing what was taking place came over and said, "Oh, I see you have met Malakai."

Patricia answered, "Yes, we have. What a sweet little guy he is."

Malakai finally built up the courage to reply, "Pleased to meet you, Mrs. Patricia. My name is Malakai, and I am eight years old."

The director suggested Malakai, Patricia and Timothy have a seat and get more acquainted. Nothing was said between Malakai and Mrs. Patricia for a few minutes. Mrs. Patricia reached into her purse and pulled out a reindeer Christmas ornament and handed it to Malakai. It was a brown reindeer with a red glittery nose and fit perfectly in his hand.

Mrs. Patricia asked Malakai, "Would you like to come home with Timothy and me and become an addition to our family? I am not sure what you are thinking or feeling Malakai, but I feel like you belong in our family."

Malakai without hesitation answered, "Yes! I would love to go home with you."

Mrs. Patricia exclaimed, "Oh! I am so happy, Malakai, and please call me Patricia. I have to go take care of a few things with the director, so you can come home with us. Please stay here and talk with Timothy."

She planted a kiss on Malakai's forehead and walked into the director's office. A short time went by, and Mrs. Patricia with her radiant smile said to Malakai, "Grab your things. You get to come home with us." Malakai did not move.

With all eyes on him, he said, "I am ready. I do not have anything else."

"Well, Malakai, we will just have to change that." Mrs. Patricia grabbed Malakai's hand, and with Mr. Timothy on the other side, they started walking toward the exit. Malakai thought, *Is this really happening to me?* Malakai, smiling from ear to ear, looked up at Mrs. Patricia and said, "Thank you."

The drive to the house seemed to take only a minute, even though it was an hour. Everything seemed more vibrant; then, Malakai envisioned the world. The house was on a beautiful street named Velardo Dr. Each house seemed to stand on its own hill like royalty. There were trees and Christmas lights paving the way to the house. Lights glistened through the bushes. Every house on the street was decorated with red, green, blue and white lights. Some houses even had blown up decorations on the yards. Malakai could not believe his eyes. He was so amazed at how magical everything looked and made him feel.

"We are home, Malakai," Mrs. Patricia said. "Let's get you settled in tonight, and tomorrow we will go Christmas tree shopping." Malakai had never had a Christmas before. He already loved Mrs. Patricia; she had such an outgoing, loving personality.

The house sat back about two hundred feet from the street. It was surrounded by a big garden of flowers and trees. It was a two-story home painted green with white shutters on every window. The front door was tall and almost all glass. On it hung a big green reef. Mrs. Patricia grabbed Malakai's hand and said, "Come on, Malakai. Let me show you your new home."

The house smelled of fresh strawberries and cinnamon. There was beautiful church-like music playing. To the left was a beautiful curved stairway. To the right was a very elaborate office with all dark cherry furniture.

"This is where Timothy spends all his time. He is an investment banker." Mrs. Patricia rolled her eyes sarcastically. Everything in the house was so intricate and elegant. Malakai was overjoyed by everything. "Let's go check out your room, Malakai." Mrs. Patricia led Malakai up the stairs. Once they reached the top, his bedroom was directly in front of the staircase. The room was colorful. There was a loose pattern of blues and greens but no theme. It was a mixture of new, vintage and homemade furniture. The room made Malakai feel inspired. It was everything he could have ever asked for. He released Mrs. Patricia's hand and ran over to the bed and plopped himself down, lay back and smiled.

"I am glad you are pleased with your room, Malakai." Mrs. Patricia walked over to the tall standing dresser and pulled out dark blue pajamas with yellow tractors on them. She placed them on the end of the bed next to Malakai. "I think these should fit. Get dressed, and when you are done, let me know." She placed another kiss on his forehead and shut the door behind her. Malakai picked up the pajamas and hugged them. They smelled like flowers, just like Mrs. Patricia. He just sat there for a few minutes taking in the new sounds and loving everything about his new home. In that very moment, Malakai felt like he had something to call his own. His very own room. Malakai started getting dressed. He noticed there was an alarm clock on the nightstand next to the bed. It read eight p.m. In the orphanage, that was the time they were to have the lights out and go to bed.

Malakai was tired, and his bed looked very comfortable. He pulled the blankets down and got into bed. The blankets were so soft and fluffy compared to the sheets he used to sleep on. Malakai placed his little reindeer ornament Mrs. Patricia gave him under his pillow. There was a little brown teddy bear on the bed. Malakai grabbed and held that teddy bear very tightly. He was so happy and at peace. His eyelids were getting heavy, and he fell right to sleep. Mrs. Patricia grew worried when Malakai did not come downstairs. She checked on him in the room and saw he was sleeping. She walked over to the bed and tucked the blankets around him tightly and softly whispered, "Good night, sweetheart. Welcome home."

Morning came, and Malakai opened his eyes forgetting where he was. He woke all frantic, and he ran out of the room crying. "Mrs. Patricia!!! Mrs. Patricia!!" He spotted her at the end of the hallway, and he ran up to her giving her a big tight hug, burying his face in her stomach. Mrs. Patricia ran her hand over Malakai's head. "It's okay, Malakai. I am right here." Malakai did not know why but her voice instantly made him feel safe. "Now, I want you to go get dressed. We have to go get a Christmas tree today. After all, it is Christmas Eve." Malakai ran back to his room and got dressed. He was so excited. A Christmas tree, wow.

It was a frosty, chilly day. Malakai, Patricia and Timothy went to the local Christmas tree farm in hopes of finding the perfect tree. Mr. Timothy put Malakai on his shoulders. Malakai's eyes gazed in excitement at all the trees and lights. Mrs. Patricia was smiling and pointing to all the trees, but none of them were quite good enough for Malakai's first Christmas with them. With their bones starting to chill to the bone, they were starting to think they were not going to find the perfect tree. Finally, at the furthest part of the farm, Mrs. Patricia spotted the perfect tree. It stood six feet tall and was the fullest tree they had seen. It was the greenest of green. Malakai thought it was perfect. Mr. Timothy took Malakai off his shoulders and started chopping down the tree. Mr. Timothy wrapped the tree in a net and dragged it to the truck.

Once they get home, Mrs. Patricia started opening boxes and inside were tree ornaments of all different kinds, big ones, small ones, red, blue, green, white and even sparkly ones. Malakai thought they all were enchanting. Malakai and his new parents gently placed all the ornaments on the tree. Malakai felt like he belonged there, and he thought the tree was the most beautiful thing he had ever seen. Malakai remembered Mrs. Patricia had given him a reindeer ornament, and it was upstairs under his pillow. He ran upstairs to grab it, and he placed in on the tree. Malakai thought to himself, *This is really what a family feels like.* They all stood back with their arms around each other admiring the tree. Malakai felt so loved and so wanted. Mrs. Patricia looked over to Malakai and asked, "What would you like for

Christmas?" Malakai looked up at Mr. Timothy and Mrs. Patricia and said, "I do not want or need anything else. I have all I need right here. This is the best gift I could have ever asked for- a family and a home to call my own!"

About the Author

Misty Hamby is thirty-one years old and was born in Redlands, California on September 14, 1984. She was raised in Yucaipa, California and is the oldest of four siblings. She graduated from Yucaipa High School early at the age of sixteen with honors and a 4.0 GPA. She was chosen for a college scholarship to Summit Career College where she studied and attained a certificate in Business Administration. She is a licensed CPA. She currently has three children: Gavin, age 10, Kierra, age 8, and Sianna Rose, age 7 months. Her children are her world. She is currently enrolled at Crafton Hills College, completing her Bachelor's degree in Business Administration. She hopes to, within the next two years, open her own accounting firm providing services, such as taxes, payroll and bookkeeping.

Edited by Dr. C. White-Elliott

Dreams
are not
Always Dreams

Lena Lebada

"This life, which had been the tomb of his virtue and of his honour, is but a walking shadow; a poor player that struts and frets his hour upon the stage, and then is heard no more: it is a tale told by an idiot, full of sound and fury, signifying nothing."
-William Shakespeare

Once there was a young boy whose name was Tom. It was mid-December, and the snow had just started falling. He was fascinated by stories and myths all his life. When Tom was still a child, he used to love all kinds of stories, from *A Christmas Carol* to *Rudolph the Red-Nosed Reindeer*. He hoped one day he could transform made-up tales into reality and live through them. So, Tom came up with an idea that maybe if he grew up and became a scientist, he could make them a reality. He was convinced that one day it would become a possibility, and he could live his dreams.

One day, Tom got dressed in his navy blue shirt and khaki pants and grabbed his little backpack that had a few shreds of old drawings. He put on his ripped up shoes and ran to the kitchen. He sat down on a brown wooden chair and waited for his mother to finish making his breakfast. His mother toasted the frozen waffles and handed him the last bit of syrup they had. He took the plate from his mom and sat down again staring at his waffles afraid that if he ate them he would not have anything left to eat for the rest of the day. Luckily, his mom gave him her lunch for the day, saying she was not that hungry. After he finished the waffles, his hands were sticky from the syrup, so he grabbed a small yellow washcloth and wiped his hands. He got up and sat in the car waiting for his mom to drive him to school.

Tom was excited to start another school day with his friends. His science teacher used to be a marine biologist, until one day she lost a few fingers while taming a shark. His sixth grade teacher loved to teach other people about wild life, and Tom loved to listen to her. He was so excited because one day he wanted to become a scientist and change what reality was. Tom walked into the colorful classroom and took a seat in the front row. He looked around at the bright paper Mache Christmas decorations hanging from the ceiling. Robin, his teacher, stood up from her bright red desk and walked toward him in her white Christmas sweater and slightly worn black skirt; she stopped at his desk and kneeled down.

She said, "Tom, I was wondering if you could stay a little bit after class." Tom was worried because he did not know what it could be regarding; he was too worried to focus for the rest of the class.

As he stared at the clock, the bell finally rang, and Tom shook with fear. Tom put his notebook in his ripped blue backpack. Then, he stood up and walked to his teacher's desk. Robin looked at him for a moment and said, "I need to talk to you about dozing off in class. It seems as if you are always tired or not interested in learning anymore." Tom looked at his teacher's face and observed her saggy face and bushy eyebrows.

"I'm just tired. That's all," said Tom in a hushed whisper. Robin slowly stood up and sighed. Then, she dismissed him. Tom left the room hoping to find a way to please himself and his mother. He used to have such good grades and was determined to work hard again.

He walked down the hallway and out the rusted blue door. He walked down the steps full of snow to his mom's red minivan that was on the verge of falling apart. His mom watched him get into the car and close the door. Then, she turned back to focus on the snowy road. She started the ignition; the drive to their house was about twenty minutes. Once they reached the freeway, his mom started with her daily interrogation of what he had accomplished in school that day. His mom asked, "So, how was your day?"

"Oh, it was fine. I was just a bit tired today," Tom replied. Then, his mom looked at him curiously.

"Are you sick? Are you dizzy or nauseous?" his mom asked.

"No, I just didn't sleep well." His mom was very worried because she did not have money to spend on medication. They did not really have any money to spend on anything other than food. She focused her eyes on the icy road and made sure to be careful because she was switching lanes. Tom all of a sudden felt a slight bump and saw nothing but pitch-black darkness.

He was frightened and did not know how to respond to the sudden darkness; all he could do was wait. Then, all of a sudden, he saw some sort of horse with a red nose; it looked just like Rudolph. He was frightened and excited at the same time. Then, he stood up and walked toward the reindeer and climbed on. The reindeer jerked a bit and then started to gallop. It took him out of the darkness and into a bright light. He closed his eyes then opened them again and saw a beautiful forest and a beautiful girl walking down a path. She was small child who looked like she was in the spirit of Christmas; he steered the reindeer toward the girl and got closer to her. Then, he saw some sort of strange-cloaked person walking towards them from the forest. He got a small glimpse of the cloaked person lurking in the shadows; it was a woman who had long brown hair and such dark green eyes.

He quickly realized the cloaked person was coming for the child, so Tom hoisted her onto the horse. He pushed the horse to its limits and went as fast as possible. Once he reached a land that was safe, he got off the horse and looked back at the child, except she was not there. She must have fallen off or was taken by the cloaked stranger. All of a sudden, it became so bright he could not make out any object surrounding him. He squinted and saw that the object in front of him was his mom. He smiled and tried to move his arms, but for some reason, he could not move them. He tried again, then once more, but they would not move. Then, his mom looked at him. He could tell from her eyes that something was extremely wrong.

A doctor walked into the room a few moments later. She looked at him and said, "I'm glad to see you awake." The doctor looked strangely familiar to him. He had seen her eyes somewhere before. His mom looked different to him. She was older and had more gray hair than he remembered. Then, a man walked into the room. He was tall and looked very strong. He had a defined jawline, but his eyes were droopy and sad.

"What happened? Why am I in here?" said Tom.

His mom looked at him and was about to speak, but her eyes welled up with tears. Tom was very worried at that point because his mom had never cried in front of him before. He soon realized the man standing with her was his father whom he had only seen a few times because he was away on military duty. Tom looked at the doctor's hand as she put her wooden clipboard down and realized she didn't have all her fingers. The doctor pulled up a rusted chair.

She sat down, leaned in and said, "Tom, this is going to be hard for you, but you were in a car accident about three years ago, and you have suffered some injuries from the crash. You seem to have a spinal cord injury, and you are paralyzed."

His mom did not say anything; she sat down feeling guilty because she had not received any major injuries from the accident. The doctor leaned in once again and said, "I'm surprised you do not remember me. It's not the first time we have bumped into each other." Tom stared at the doctor and realized she had an uncanny resemblance to the cloaked woman and his teacher. He finally realized the woman was Scrooge. He soon realized that living your dream does not mean it will be the way you dreamed it to be, and reality is not always what you thought it was.

About the Author

Lena Lebada has a few hobbies, including playing the flute and the piano, drawing and writing. She is a college student and hopes to pursue a career in the medical field.

A Sinful ~~Bourbon~~ Christmas

Burbank

Jade Lopez-Spence

"Lots of people want to ride with you in the limo, but what you want is someone who will take the bus with you when the limo breaks down."
-Oprah Winfrey

Let me start off by explaining my origin. I grew up in the Coachella Valley, a small community with similar faces everywhere you turn. Living in a big city was always a fantasy of mine. Before I get ahead of myself, let me formally introduce myself. My name is Adelaide Gomez-Lorenz. (I know it's a mouthful.) I moved to the greatest city in America: Los Angeles: the city of dreams and opportunities. For two years, I developed the strangest friendships, and it was customary to have certain individuals present during "turn ups," or parties as one would say.

One amongst them was a friend turned roommate and fellow classmate: Torie Lashey. Torie was the Mother Teresa of the group. She was all sugar, no spice and everything nice, proven by her lack of alcohol soaked liver- before she met me. Then, there is Macey Light, the Libra. She was a force of unstoppable energy. Macey Light was up for anything. There was no mountain too tall for that girl, which is the exact opposite to her beau, Smokey Johnson. He didn't exactly get his name from the forest fire commercial "Smokey Bear." Smokey was a bonafide pothead, a Maryjane-loving person. That brings me to Smokey's best friend, Daron Danes (Pothead #2). The duo was bonded by the potent green herbs they craved every day. Last, but not least, is Gilberto Castilla. The hyper-induced Aries was the oldest amongst us. He was the procurer; in simple terms, he bought the booze. But, he had his own vice he hid under his swag-- much stronger than marijuana. Another topic for another story though. They weren't perfect law-abiding citizens, but my friends made life interesting.

It was December 2014, and the air was dry and cold, as cold

as a California winter could be. I was sitting at home with absolutely nothing to do, when I realized it had been months since I last saw the group. Earlier that summer, I had moved back to my hometown in the Coachella Valley.

I found myself lost in papers of assignments and working almost every day. It was time to put life on pause and revisit the past. The first thing I did was call my good friend Torie. From there, I contacted the rest of the group. That Christmas, we would all meet up in Burbank, California.

The day finally came, and I had everything set up. The hotel was booked and bottles of bourbon, gin and tequila were all present. I heard three knocks on the door while planning to jump in the shower to get ready. Sure enough it was Macey, Smokey, and Daron; my three favorite potheads were the first to arrive. The trio was nearly out of breath and dripping with sweat, caused by the afternoon sun. They had walked a few good miles from Bus Stop 22 to get to the Burbank Hotel. One by one, they each filed in. "What's good?!" Macey huffed. All I could do was smile and look distinctively in the direction of where the bottles of alcohol lay. Macey smiled back and said, "Let's get drinking." A custom ritual of pre-turn up events is for the females to get dressed and look good. So that's exactly what Macey and I did- get ready. As soon as we were all freshly showered, bottles were cracked open and the first round of shots was taken.

I was on shot number four when my phone vibrated. Gilberto had blown up my phone texting and asking about the location of the hotel. Completely focused on the Bourbon bottle, I passed my phone to Macey to address him. A whole hour passed by before we heard a knock at the door. I slowly trampled to the door already buzzing from several shades of liquor. The person who stood before me was a resemblance of Gilberto Castilla. He had lost so much weight since I had last seen him. I had to blink several times to make sure the pod-person was he. The man who stood at the door had an easy sly smile on his face with slightly furrowed brows. Gilberto had finally arrived. I welcomed him in as the group was taking more shots. Macey ran to hug him as I was still shocked by the loss of his extra pounds. We had all known Gilberto to be huskily built. He had always been as Macey put it "Sexy Chunky." Finally snapping out of my daze, I rejoined the group.

It was midnight when I realized there was one more person missing: Torie. I checked my phone, and there were several text messages and missed calls from her. I quickly called her back. She picked up and said, "Go downstairs." Confused but ready, I gathered my shoes and hurried downstairs. A bright green Uber car pulled up to the entrance of the hotel and out poured Torie. I hugged her immediately and helped her with her things. "Finally, you're here," I said. "I almost didn't make it," she replied. We raced up the stairs to the hotel room. I opened the door for my friend, and everyone welcomed her with big open arms.

Torie's arrival meant the little gathering had finally started. Technically, half the group was already buzzed, including me. Regardless, I took shots with a sober Torie and an eager Gilberto. Hours passed by when pod Gilberto started to shout, "Body Shots!" Torie shied away and said, "Oh, God no." Macey and Smokey chimed in and agreed with Gilberto. Not realizing I would be the first victim, I supported the group's events. Gilberto quickly shouted, "Adelaide and Macey." I sighed long and deep as I got up from the comfort of the hotel bed and faced Macey. That night was the first time I did a body shot, and to say the least, it was weird. However, it was extremely funny when I spilled tequila on Macey by failing to consume the whole shot on her chest. Our little Torie was next as Gilberto volunteered her to be paired with Macey. Only her fate was far more dangerous. Macey got down on all four and arched her back in preparation for the shot to be placed on top. Gilberto declared that Torie must take an ass shot. Macey smiled and replied, "Don't worry. It's clean. I took a shower." We all laughed hard as Torie completed the challenge.

The night proceeded as Macey thought about the next ridiculous event to take place. Strip poker was chosen! By the time Macey decided the game however, the two potheads had fallen asleep. The participants would be Macey, Gilberto, Torie and myself included. Even buzzed Torie would have limits to how far she was willing to go in strip poker. It would be Gilberto, Macey and I doing the liberation of clothing. By round two, Torie had won again, and I was left with the bottom half of my dress pushed down. My arms lay constructively against my chest as I covered up.

The third game approached, and all of us were half naked in our underwear, except for a determined Torie. I had lost all bets at that point. Left only in my lace underwear, I kept my arms folded and crouched beside the bed. Suddenly jerked up on my feet by an eager Gilberto, stunned I stayed frozen as I watched Gilberto speak to Macey. "Look at this," Gilberto explained by spanking me and grabbing my ass. "Macey, my ninja, you gotta kick him off the bed," Gilberto said as he jerked his head toward a sleeping Daron. Macey quickly pulled me to the side of the hotel's bathroom and asked, "Do you want him?" I gasped overwhelmed by the night's events. "I just want my sleep," I said, shrugging off the idea of Gilberto.

We returned to where a sleepy Torie sat and to Gilberto standing and waiting. Macey quickly got Daron off the second bed where he had fallen asleep and help relocate him to the hotel's carpeted floor. Gilberto, finally getting the green light, grabbed me and guided me to the bed. I could not see his face because the light was shut off, but I could tell he had expectations for the night. He turned towards me and was ready to make a move when Torie, already drunk, stumbled across the room and flopped down in between us. Torie talked for the whole night half asleep and half buzzed about life in general and relationships. I couldn't hide the smile on my face as I heard the annoyed tone in Gilberto's voice as he groaned over Torie's rants. So there we lay, the three of us in one queen-sized bed smooched together, as Macey and her beau lay in the next bed and a still high Daron lay on the floor.

The night sped by as we all lay in bed. Christmas was nearly over, and everyone was either drunk, high or in between. I wasn't worried about my family back home because I knew they were okay. I would not change how my Christmas turned out in the world. My little pack of friends is the family I chose to spend the holidays with. Even with all their flaws, I loved them. "Merry Christmas, Weirdoes," I whispered as the night came to an end. 'Til the next reunion.

About the Author

Raised in the Coachella Valley in Southern California, Jade Lopez-Spence was raised by her mother's family, having lost her mother at the age of fifteen. This young charismatic artist had a passion to create and design. That passion led her to move to the great city of Los Angeles to study fashion design for two years. Los Angeles felt like home to the young dreamer, and it's where she experienced the best and worst times that led her to meet the most fascinating people.

Edited by Dr. C. White-Elliott

The Gift Worth Giving

Miguel Montes

"I have found that among its other benefits,
giving liberates the soul of the giver."
-Maya Angelou

Cold and quiet, the corridors never seemed so lonely. If it weren't for the night sky shedding light through the stained windows, Sabrina would not have been able to write in her journal. It was about the only thing that gave her freedom. Freedom to wonder, freedom to imagine, freedom to dream. Ironic, because while every other girl was sleeping, dreaming away, hopefully of a better place than that, Sabrina dreamt differently. She figured that was the only way to hold onto her dreams, instead of being disappointed every time when she awakened to realize they weren't real. Sabrina very much wanted those dreams to be alive.

The holidays were just around the corner. So that time, she was writing of a winter wonderland, which consisted of everything from houses draped in Christmas lights, carolers singing cheerful tunes, tall Christmas trees with presents nestled at the bottom, and lastly, all the holiday cooking you could imagine. Sabrina was getting carried away with her thoughts when all of a sudden, she heard footsteps coming down the hall. In a hasty response, she put her journal back underneath her bed, then acted as if she were asleep. There was only one person walking around at that time of the night: Ms. Hader, secretly known around the orphanage as "Ms. Hate-her."

She was the orphanage director, a short and sturdy woman, with piercing eyes that could stop a train in its tracks. She had jet black hair that was always tied up tightly in a bun, and believe me when I say that she wasn't the most stylish person. Still, don't let the appearance of that woman fool you, because what she lacked in size, she demanded in authority.

Ms. Hader grew particularly moody around Christmas time. It was said it was due to never having a family of her own. That was one of the reasons why girls seemed to stick around a little longer than usual in that place.

Her heels were clicking-and-clacking closer towards Sabrina's direction. It wouldn't be her first time catching Sabrina awake past curfew. If anything, she expected it. But that time, Sabrina happened to slide right under her nose. As Ms. Hader slowly descended back to her room, Sabrina made one last attempt to finish up where she had left off in her journal. She had to finish up her dream Christmas before she fell asleep to wake up to another nightmare.

In the last entry of her journal, Sabrina eloquently wrote, "It has been quite some time since I've last enjoyed a Christmas worth celebrating. I mean, since I lost Mom and Dad, it's made times like these a little more difficult, and living in this place doesn't help. I just want to spread Christmas joy this year, not just for myself, but for all the other girls who have lost hope in Christmas here in this orphanage. Isn't that what Christmas is all about? Giving?" She then closed her journal and peacefully fell asleep.

Ding, Dong, Ding, Dong! "Rise and shine, ladies. We've got a long day ahead of us!" Ms. Hader usually woke up all the girls in that sort of military fashion, but today she seemed a little bit on the bright side.

"Come on now, girls! Hurry up! I've got a surprise for you," Ms. Hader said in almost of a tune.

"Whoa, what's up with Hate-her today?! Is it me, or is she acting a little weird?" asked Jewel, another girl at the orphanage.

"Who knows?" replied Sam.

"Maybe, it's just another trick to get us to go work again like last time," added Jewel.

"Relax guys. I mean who knows. Maybe she has some gifts for us. Christmas is coming up you know," Sabrina said in hopes that the girls would agree. Instead, all at once, the girls began to laugh.

"Oh, please! Tell me you don't believe that Sabrina," Sam said.

"It's been so long. I've already forgotten how it was to celebrate Christmas," Jewel replied, in what seemed to be a joking manner.

"Seriously, guys. I truly believe that Ms. Hader has gotten into the Christmas spirit this year," Sabrina responded optimistically.

"Whatever you say!" said Sam.

So, as the girls stumbled out of their bunk beds, they were eager to see what the surprise was all about. Ms. Hader made them line up in two single-file lines and directed them out of the orphanage home. It was cold and cloudy that morning, with a slightly chilled breeze that caressed the young girls' faces as soon as they stepped outside. The sign outside the orphanage read, "New Hope Orphanage." Every time Sabrina saw that sign, she always wondered how she got there. It always brought back memories about how her life was before the orphanage.

They were then at the front, almost near the road that led to the entrance of the orphanage. You could see the confusion on all the girls' faces. Ms. Hader had never let them get that far away from the vicinity. Ms. Hader got in front of the crowd of bewildered girls and began to say, "Alright now, ladies. You are all probably wondering why I've pulled you out this far. Well, the truth is I have arranged for a trip into town, so we can go and be a part of the holiday spirit." In utter shock, the girls remained silent for a few seconds. "Well, aren't you girls going to say something?" After Ms. Hader said that, all the girls broke out into cheer. Some laughing in joy, high fiving each other, and some so happy they burst into tears. For once, Sabrina felt like there was hope in that place. Maybe a new hope.

As the bus came and picked up the girls, they all couldn't wait to get on and enjoy the day ahead of them. On the whole ride into town, which took about forty-five minutes, they were singing Christmas songs. "Jingle bells, jingle bells, jingle all the way..." In the midst of all the cheerful singing, Sabrina happened to take a look at Ms. Hader and witnessed the biggest smile she had ever seen on her face since living at the orphanage. It made her feel nice and warm inside. Then, she began to wonder what the whole thing was all about. What was it that changed Ms. Hader?

When they finally got into town, they were amazed at all the lights and Christmas ornaments being displayed. It really brought a smile to every single one of those girls' faces. Everyone was such in the holiday spirit. As soon as they got off the bus, the girls scattered into the streets in excitement. Ms. Hader, in a worried voice, yelled out, "Watch yourself, girls! Make sure you look both ways when crossing the street!" It surprised Sabrina to see Ms. Hader acting in a calm manner. I guess you can say the old Ms. Hader wouldn't have been so fond of that sort of attitude. Sabrina committed herself to help Ms. Hader out the rest of the trip, primarily because she wanted to see if she could figure out why Ms. Hader was acting the way she was. Not like it was a bad thing, but just because she was curious.

So, along they went. Ms. Hader and Sabrina immediately kicked it off. They began by buying Christmas decorations for the orphanage: lights, ornaments, stockings, and anything you could imagine that would make Christmas, Christmas. Everything was almost complete, but they were still missing one thing: a Christmas tree. So, off they went. When they came across the tree they wanted, it was a unanimous decision. It was like all the girls were looking at the same tree. It was a big, beautiful green Christmas tree. Ms. Hader said it was perfect because it was big enough for the whole orphanage. It took the help of some burley townsmen to get the tree the girls wanted inside the bus, but they pulled it off.

On the ride back to the orphanage, Sabrina sat right next to Ms. Hader and continued their discussion until they were back. As they were talking, Sabrina was trying to muster up the courage to ask Ms. Hader why she was acting the way she was. She didn't want it to come out in a bad way.

"Umm, Ms. Hader, may I add that I think it's a wonderful thing what you're doing today for all of us here at the orphanage. But I have to ask, 'Why?'"

Ms. Hader laughed, "Oh, Sabrina, I know I've been hard on you girls for quite some time now, and to be honest with you, I can't explain why." Tears began to trickle from Ms. Hader's eyes.

"When I became the director here at the orphanage, I was going through some tough times in my personal life. You see, I dedicated my whole life to helping people. So much that I didn't even get the time to have a family of my own. Then, something terrible happened: I lost my parents."

Sabrina began to tear up because it brought back memories of how she had lost her parents.

Ms. Hader continued, "My parents meant the world to me. I became so angry at the world because I wasn't there to help my parents when they were in need of my assistance. I was always busy helping others. I felt like I could've done something to prevent their death, but the truth was I couldn't. I became selfish and began to hold a grudge because of that. It made me into a bitter person."

The bus was already getting close to their destination, and Sabrina felt like she and Ms. Hader had made a real good connection. Ms. Hader wiped her tears then said, "Look at me. I'm a mess." They both began to laugh. Then she continued, "Sabrina, I'm really glad we had this talk. I guess I lost sense of who I really was, and what I was put on this earth for." The bus driver pulled into the driveway of the orphanage then yelled, "Alright, ladies. We're home!"

Once all the girls got settled in, they began to decorate the place. You had never seen so much joy on their faces until that day. Everyone was doing her part to bring some Christmas cheer to the orphanage. Ornaments were hanging from everywhere, lights were being wrapped around the poles of the bunk beds, and stockings were being pinned where ever the girls pleased. They saved the best part for last, which was the Christmas tree.

Ms. Hader picked a perfect spot to place the tree, in the living-room right near the fireplace. Everyone was pleased about how the placed looked and called it a day.

Ms. Hader had an announcement to make before everyone went to bed. She made sure to gather up all the girls, then she began by saying, "Alright, girls. Now Christmas is still about a week away, so we got to start planning what we want to make to eat for this Christmas. So if anyone has suggestions, make sure to write them down. Okay?"

"Oh, sweet!" one of the girls replied in excitement. Ms. Hader began to walk towards Sabrina, while she was getting ready for bed. When she got there, she asked, "Sabrina, do you mind helping me place the star on top of the Christmas tree?"

"Of course," Sabrina answered.

As they were making their way to the living room, Sabrina said, "It's going to be a great Christmas this year!"

Ms. Hader replied back, "It sure is."

"I wanted to ask," Sabrina said, "What made you choose Christmas to begin this transformation?"

Ms. Hader was grabbing the ladder to put the star on the tree when she said, "Well, Christmas is the season of giving right? I felt like I needed to give back to you girls in a big way, and it's not about the gifts or any of that. It's about love, respect, and appreciation. Now, that's a gift worth giving." It was then and there when Sabrina realized what the true meaning of Christmas really was, and from then on, *New Hope Orphanage* never had a bad Christmas again.

About the Author

Born in Indio, California, Miguel Montes is a 25-year-old Hispanic male. Raised by a single mother, he is the oldest of three siblings. He and his younger brother are first-generation college students. He is currently in his second year at College of the Desert and hopes to transfer to UC Berkeley. His career goal is to become an attorney at law. He dedicates this short story to his little sister Sabrina Selena Montes.

Edited by Dr. C. White-Elliott

REFLECTIONS
IN AN
UNEXPECTED
PLACE

Ana Y. Quintana

"We always seek and rarely find. You need not go too far, just let the reflections reveal the truths inside."

-Ana Y. Quintana

She looked back at her reflection in the mirror. Perhaps being accustomed to seeing that optimistic bright-eyed girl staring back at her, she didn't realize the confidence had drifted away. The confidence that kept her warm and inspired her lovely experiences for so long had disappeared. What remained was an unremarkable woman. Her bright green eyes with yellow shades and dark blue ring, smiled no longer, appearing empty and holding fast to a distant sadness as an anchor of hope.

"Could he be right? . . . How did this happen? . . . Why did I let this happen?" were just a few questions that plagued her mind, after his honest and raw observation.

Evelyn, like most twenty-something-year olds, was a school-aholic and lacked balance. She pushed herself to a point that a break was a must. After graduating from college, she packed up her life into her parents' van and moved back home. It was time to start a new chapter.

But what if what I think I want isn't what I need or truly want? she asked herself as she said goodbye to the lovely memories that shaped so much the person she was.

Like most fresh starts, something new and something small was a must. Evelyn thought a small lower-level marketing job fit that exact bill. *This new gig is only temporary. My goal is to figure out if what I WANT to do is actually what I am MEANT to do. In the meantime, I will met new people and learn some new skills,* she thought to herself.

Four years later . . .

How did a short break become a four-year break? Ugh, I'm no closer to figuring out what path than I was then. A sign from above would be nice, guys! she thought as she looked at the distant blue skies.

One morning in early-December 2014, the Christmas air thickened with the desert winds and endless sands. Evelyn buttoned down her long dark purple coat, slipped her fingers in her black gloves, and placed her vibrant hippy-colored purse across her shoulders, so it would fall directly at her hips. It was 6am, and the sun was barely rising.

That day, she was running late and could not miss her bus to town. As she was about to bike downhill, she had an overwhelming feeling of uncertainty overcome her. As she reflected on the sensation, she smiled and remembered to buckle her helmet under her chin and turn on all her lights. *Gotta protect that money maker!* she laughed to herself as she tapped her helmet.

As she rode downhill, her speed appeared to increase unexpectedly. Evelyn had forgotten to change her gears back to one. Two likely scenarios crossed her thoughts if she suddenly hit her breaks - she would be safe or fly forward. The thought of crashing into a row of cacti in her direct line of sight did not make her situation any better. The adrenaline began to pump through every inch of her arteries and that enchanting Spanish yellow house with lovely large cacti with ever so pointy thorns called out to her. As if they were welcoming her to a dire fate of pain, her stomach twisted a little further in anticipation.

She looked left, right, and left again before making a sharp left on her bike and barely missing the cacti. "Muhahaha, beautiful cacti with lovely Christmas flowers, today I will not become your next prey!" But, she laughed too soon. She quickly lost balance of her bike and already going at a high speed, she flipped into the adjacent neighbor's bushes. So, there she laid on the ground trying to make sense of her current mental fog. Her purple coat was covered with dirt and leaves. It happened so quickly that she was still unsure of how exactly she flipped the bike. But one thing was certain - she did not have the last laugh. She detangled her legs from her bike and lifted herself from the ground. *So this is what an adrenaline rush feels like? Ugh, my foot is covered in blood, and my knee is so swollen,* she thought as her eyes widened, looking at her left leg.

"Hey, Dad? I had an accident. Can you come get me?" she nervously asked over the phone. Her father arrived a few minutes later. He placed her bike into the car and helped her slowly into her seat. "Kiddo, looks like you did a number on that knee. Let me drop off your bike at the house, and we can head straight to the emergency room," her father said calmly.

A few weeks later...
"What's the address again?" her father asked as they searched for her physical therapist's address.
"2016 Crossroads Drive," she replied.
"There it is- Clear Skies Physical Therapy! It is to my left," her father said.

What a peculiar street address, she thought to herself as she swung her crutches to the front door. "Hello, my name is Evelyn. I have a 10am appointment," she said pleasantly to the girl behind the lobby desk, who was dolled up with Christmas greens and bright red sweater. As she waited, Evelyn glared at the large 18-foot-mirrored wall dividing the lobby from the workout area. She could see five tables off in the distance behind the wall and workout machines to the far right of the tables. Once seated, her attention drifted back to the mirrored wall and her own reflection. Her thoughts of nothing merged with her everyday thoughts. There were so many emotions and detachments begging for comforted attention that she chose to submerge herself in a sea of them all.

In a moment of pure vulnerability and solace, she found herself asking her reflection, "Mirror mirror on the wall, what secrets do you hold from me?" She paused and chuckled as she continued staring directly at those emerald green eyes. "A little hint and guidance would be nice."

"Dr. Harper will be with you shortly," said the receptionist gingerly at a distance. Time became infinite as she consumed herself in deep thought. She had not noticed a deep voice calling out her name. "Nickels for your thoughts, love?" said a tall handsome fellow while tapping her on her shoulder. His English accent caught her attention as their eyes immediately met.

She paused for a few seconds and stared at his beautiful clear blue eyes and long red eyelashes. There was an overwhelming warmth and kindness in his eyes, and at the same time, a perplexing deep sorrow hid in the shadows. Evelyn stood up, smiled, and extended her hand towards him. "You might be here a wee bit," she replied jokingly. "I am sorry; it has been a busy week. I am Evelyn. You must be Dr. Harper," she said with a firm but welcoming handshake.

As he led her into the consultation room, her eyes sparked with interest at all the skeletal drawings and diagrams of the human body on the walls. He noticed but remained silent. He continued the examination with thorough questions about her accident, pain, and mobility. Evelyn took advantage of his warm and comforting nature to pick his brain.

"Could you explain to me what happened structure wise with my knee during the accident? And please no need to simplify the explanation. I'm a quick study," she stated with a smile.

Perhaps taken aback by her curiosity or direct questioning, he responded in length with full medical terminology in hand. When he finished explaining and pointing to the many diagrams, Evelyn paused and cocked her head slightly to the right. She was processing every word he had said and trying to visually imagine her ligaments and muscles at work right before and during the accident. He perhaps thought he lost her with his jargon, but she just smiled back at him. Evelyn was no dumb broad and had been for some time reading medical and scientific journals for fun.

"Could my knee pain or intensity of pain be caused from injury in another part of my body?" she asked.

"Of course, lower back pain can also manifest itself in the knee," he responded in an intrigued and surprised tone from her inquiry. "Well, that's all for today. Please make an appointment with my secretary for your follow up."

"Sure thing, Dr. Harper. Thank you again for answering my questions by the way. I have a tendency to ask a lot of questions," she chuckled as she extended her hand.

"Of course, anytime. Call me Roger, please. And Merry Christmas!" he said as he shook her hand.

In her following visits, Evelyn took notice of the doctor who was treating her. There was an instant gravitational energy between them. She did not dare to contemplate his attractive physical qualities too long. *He's my doctor, and he is obviously not interested in me, nor can he be,* she told herself. *And with that said, there is no harm in observing his tall muscular shoulders, arms, and firm bum as he walks around the room*, she chuckled to herself.

Evelyn naturally felt at home at her physical therapy facility. She often would start up or jump into random conversations about science, education discrepancies, politics, and patient health issues with fellow patients and staff. She especially enjoyed speaking in Spanish to non-English speaking patients about their injuries. Her interests were pure in scientific curiosity and empathy towards seeing another person in pain.

She apparently did it often enough that Roger felt compelled to ask, "What are you doing wasting your time at that marketing office? You are too smart and should use your potential for good. Doctor, perhaps?"

"Doctor?" followed by a long pause. "It's interesting you bring that up. During my undergraduate years, I had thought about a career in medicine but thought I wasn't smart enough."

"I have two words for you - medical doctor! Have you noticed every time you come here, you are asking patients how they are feeling? How they are progressing? Asking me a million questions about one thing or another related to the human body. And, you are pretty bright for an American- now that I think about it," Roger said as they both joined in a laugh.

Evelyn remained silent, contemplating his observation for the rest of the session. She and Roger had begun to develop a strong friendship. She trusted him. She had not realized how much she needed the intellectual stimulation and encourage-ment from a peer.

Perhaps, he has a point? she thought.

In the days that followed, she noticed how random conversations with people eventually involved medicine in one way or another. *Is this strange or what? Random coincidences or intentional signs I wonder? I wonder . . . Mmmm, why not?*

When she saw Roger a few weeks later, she asked him to meet her for coffee to pick his brain. She asked her usual twenty questions under the sun and transitioned into random news-worthy issues. At one point, her mind drifted.

"Are you okay? I know you good enough to say silence is never a good thing when those wheels start turning in your head!" He laughed.

"I find myself thinking about my future a lot nowadays. Actually have been for a while," she said. She continued telling him a bit more about her passions, interests, and what her break was meant to bring her.

"What is the problem, love? Sounds like a great plan. So, I ask again, 'What is the problem?'" he said. Concern and deep thought plagued her face. "The problem is that you lost your spark. Your flame. You find yourself roaming in search of a flame that will never come unless you flick the lighter!" he exclaimed.

Could he be right? How did this happen? Why did I let this happen? she reflected. "Do you think I'm lost? Have I truly lost confidence in myself?" she asked.

"Yes." After a few second pause, he continued, "And it is perfectly okay."

"I gave my two-week notice today," she said as she stared into a rain puddle on the sidewalk outside the café.

"Really?" he asked completely shocked.

"Is that hard to believe? I want to focus my attention solely on what matters. About time, huh?" she smiled. "Ugh, I think I have been lost for a while now. I do not understand why or how I let this happen," she sighed.

"What are your plans?" he asked curiously.

"Probably buying you a box of European chocolate!" she laughed. "Did I ever tell you I made a wish on Christmas Eve?" she smiled. Roger just glared as if the notion was strange. "I asked the powers that be for guidance. I asked for a sign to help me discover my purpose. I asked for inner strength," she stated. "I crashed my bike because I was supposed to change my path. I was supposed to meet you. Maybe I was not paying attention to well to the signs before my accident," she laughed. "I realize now that my wish was already granted before I even articulated it. We were supposed to meet, you see? You were supposed to help me transition and regain my confidence again." She paused and drifted into her abstract reflection in the rain puddle.

After many moments, she smiled and looked directly into the deep blue eyes that once captivated her interest some seven months prior. She could have never expected her wish would turn her whole life around. Yet, she was finally happy and discovered the answers she had long sought after.

"I am going to medical school," she said with a smile.

About the Author

Ana Y. Quintana received her Bachelors of Science in Biology and minor in Mathematics from California State University, Monterey Bay. As a Ronald E. McNair Scholar, Ana had incredible experiences conducting genetics and molecular cellular research across the country and presenting her research in multiple academic forums, including the Society for the Advancement of Chicanos and Native Americans in Science National Conference. When Ana is not running around playing with her young niece and nephews, she is checking off boxes on her bucket list. She recently purchased a piano and is looking forward to transitioning from beginner to intermediate soon! Ana plans on continuing her education in medicine and integrating a career in medicine and public service. You can reach her at ayquintana@gmail.com.

Edited by Dr. C. White-Elliott

The Jungle's First Winter

Hector Ramirez

"Change is the law of life. And those who look towards the past or present are certain to miss the future."
-John F. Kennedy

A thick jungle of sublime beauty, white sandy beaches, the ocean turquoise in color, the sound of exotic birds chirping in the trees, flowers growing wild from left to right is a paradise treasured by the kingdom of animals that call it home. There are no defined laws in this land but instead a natural order exists, an unspoken consensus that merely happened, where the many species of this jungle get along in relative peace. This surreal land is inhabited by many animals with no single government or any dynasty that rules over them; of all the giraffes and hippos, snakes and rhinos, crocodiles and toucans, elephants and lions, only two animals were respected enough to be deemed as leaders.

The two are Elliott, the arch elephant, and Leonard, lord of the lions. Even with their conflicting views, they manage to preserve balance in the jungle. These two leaders aren't enemies but aren't best friends either and only met ceremoniously a few times a year to discuss matters concerning the jungle. A few days before the two leaders approach summit, where other animals would also gain an audience to bring up other concerns that might have previously gone unnoticed, a series of events would transpire forever changing the nature of the jungle, but it would be up to future generations to decide if it was for the better or worse.

The summit, being held on the shore, will be hosted this time by Elliott, where he and Leonard will take questions from representatives of the other animal inhabitants. It's the middle of summer, yet there's a cool wind and cloudy skies, which normally signaled rain, made today feel rather peculiar. Leonard notices this as he arrives to the shore where the summit will be held in a few days but doesn't care to mention it. "We, members of the jungle, are gathered here today to answer any and all questions that may have come up since our last summit," said the flustered Elliott having gone through much trouble organizing the event. "Blah, blah, blah. We'll start with the most common thought on everybody's mind: Who will host this year's Cornucopia event? How is that for an introduction, Leonard?"

The Cornucopia event is a gathering of the jungle where all the animals sing in organized tune and a new, original, melody is sung each year. It is the one day where all the animals come enjoy the night as a single animal kingdom. There's never a winner or loser, never a prize or trophy, but it's held for the sake of tradition and to brighten the spirits of the animals for a good year to come. It's a day all the animals of the jungle look forward to. However, before Elliott could continue planning the coming summit, Leonard spots something out in the horizon.

"Elliott...excuse the interruption...but it appears we have a guest," Leonard calmly says with his deep and powerful voice befitting for even a king. "I wasn't aware that you invited our aquatic neighbors. They're very early."

"How strange because I didn't...and believe me...I would've remembered if I had," Elliott says confusedly, wondering what the object in the distance is.

"Look. I don't even recognize it. It's far too large to be a dolphin," Leonard says as the object in question approaches closer. "It looks like it's made of wood. What are those colors hanging above it? Let's pause what we're doing for a moment and investigate."

"But...we have so much to do. I haven't even decided whether I want the seats to be arranged in a circle or an oval, let alone if we're even going to have seats."

"Exactly. Whatever that thing is it obviously isn't aware of the coming summit; otherwise, they wouldn't be arriving to the shore today of all days. Let's investigate."

Elliott becoming frustrated by this abrupt request yet did have to oblige because he knows that Leonard's comfort was a top priority as to assure that the meeting would run smoothly. So, the two rush down to the shore to get a closer view of the approaching object in hopes of greeting it--whatever it is--upon its immediate arrival. At the shore, Leonard stood up on his hind legs to get a better view. Elliott raises his big ears listening closely for a sound it might make. The object still cannot be identified and approaches slowly but surely.

"Do you hear anything?" Leonard asks with a sense of impatience.

"I hear a few voices chanting the words 'land hoe' whatever that means."

"Then, it's a floating vessel of some kind. Let's wait for whoever is on it to come to us.

So, the tall and large floating vessel, the boat, approaches as close as it can. The wood is a dark shade of brown, the sails are huge and has a crest painted on as if to show nobility or stature, and all the crew on board is standing at the edge of the boat cheering. The very sight of this boat is frightening to the two leaders because it is like nothing they had ever seen. It makes them feel small, but they knew what they represent, a beautiful jungle and all its inhabitants, so they stand there firmly, ready to formally introduce themselves.

"Ahoy! Are you animals the inhabitants here?" the odd animals of the boat yell.

No response is given to that question by the two. So, the odd animals of the large boat climb down onto smaller boats to get themselves onto the shore. These odd boat animals seem excited, at ease as they approach the shore, and look like no animal that Elliott and Leonard has ever seen. They are covered in strange colorful coats with various patterns and pockets all over. All of them are hairless, except for the tops of their heads. They look terrifying to the two.

Leonard, as bold and noble as he is, walks up to the first one to land on the shore and says, "Welcome. Allow me to introduce myself because you seem to have confused us with Ahoys. I am Leonard, lord of the lions."

"I'm the Arch Elephant Elliott. It's truly a pleasure to make your acquaintance."

"Wow, impressive titles. I am humbled. I bet you're wondering who I am. Well, unfortunately, I am not much. I am a man, and these are my fellow crewmembers, but don't mind them. I do all the talking. You probably haven't seen any men because we all live in the Northern Hemisphere mostly. I am also a travelling trader. I came here to sell Christmas! The beautiful Christmas and all its required knick-knacks. I'm sure you have all been in need of some Christmas trees, correct? Seeing that the nearest ones are in the mountains of North Carolina. Fortunately, I got you covered there! How many do you think you'll you be needing?"

Leonard and Elliott stand there, confused at the man with his fanciful garments and big smile, hearing his sales pitch about a holiday they had never heard of.

"Excuse me. I'm terribly sorry. You both don't even know what Christmas is. Correct?"

"No, we don't."

"Lots of places I've visited don't, especially in this southern Hemisphere. You're missing out. It's great! It's the only holiday you need."

"I'll have to stop you there. We already have a holiday that we're in the middle of preparing for," Leonard abruptly says with an offended look in his eyes.

"Are you? Well, hmm okay. Do you mind if my fellow crew and I stay in your jungle for a bit? We're feeling very exhausted after the long sea voyage and would appreciate resting on dry land for a few nights."

So Leonard and Elliott, not saying much else, kindly allow the man and the rest of his crew to stay for however long needed on the shore as the two resume their preparations for the Cornucopia event. But, the man has other plans in mind. He is a skilled trader and very familiar with this type of situation. He is a man that knows whom to sell to and how to sell it. So, his first step is to pique the animals' interest in his product and create a demand for Christmas where he will be the sole supplier of it.

One morning, in the jungle next to a popular riverbed where all the animals spend much of their time, the man stands up on top of a large rock with a brightly colored wrapped gift in his hand and yells, "Young jungle animals! Look at what I have in my hand." The man is soon surrounded by curious young cubs and calves, kits and kittens, fawns and piglets, and hatchling and whelps.

"I bet you're wondering what this peculiar thing is? Well, it's for you," as he hands it to a young tiger cub.

"What is it?" the cub asks with excitement while all the other little animals surrounded the young tiger in awe of the brightly colored wrapped gift.

"It's a surprise! But, you're not allowed to open it until Christmas. It's the rule," the man says with a huge charming smile, "but, I unfortunately don't have many to give out because there isn't enough Christmas in this jungle."

"How do we get more Christmas?" the young tiger cub asks.

The man smiles and proceeds to explain Christmas in all its glory to all the young animals at the riverbank. He tells them about the beauty and role of the Christmas tree, the sock stockings and what socks are, the mistletoe and what kisses are, the Christmas gift and what exactly a gift is supposed to be. The news of this holiday spreads like wildfire, metaphorically because a wildfire in a jungle would be a disaster, and the excitement surprises nobody more than Leonard and Elliott. The man never bothers to explain to the two exactly what Christmas is or why they should be excited about it. So, Elliott and Leonard decide to look more into this Christmas thing at the request of the young animals' parents because the hype got them excited as well. Elliott and Leonard approach the man at his camp just at the shore not too far from his boat.

"Oh. It's you two! Requesting an audience are we?" The man says with a smile as he exits out of his tiny humble tent. "It's a bit early to be seeing you two here. To what do I owe the pleasure?"

"We've been receiving a number of requests from our fellow animals that they want more of this Christmas thing," Elliott says. "But that brings us to a dilemma because your Christmas thing falls right on our Cornucopia event. Would you mind moving it?"

"Oh no. I'm sorry. Christmas can only fall on this date. It's the rule. It looks like the only way would be for you to move your Cornucopia event," the man says with a huge frown. "Except, from what I've heard from the other animals, your Cornucopia event can only fall on this one day because of how the stars align just right once a year. How inconvenient."

"Well, I'm sure there's no harm in having a few animals miss out on our beloved hymns this year. We'll come back to you in regards to your offer as we find out how much Christmas we're going to need for the other animals," Leonard says as he walked away with Elliott.

"But, Leonard, we never miss out on a single animal. Are you sure about this?"

"What's a few voices missing out going to mean? We don't control the other animals; we only watch over them."

"I'm sorry, but I'm going to have to disagree. This holiday is far too sacred."

Leonard and Elliott argue for quite some time and eventually come to the agreement that they would decide how much Christmas the animals would get. They go around to talk to the other animals, astonished by how many of them seemed excited for it, and decide they will bargain for a third of the requested amount of Christmas. Elliott is still upset that any Christmas was being made at all for the cost of some animals missing out on the hymns, but he does believe in the value of compromise. Elliott and Leonard both wake up very early, meet at the shore, and wait outside the man's camp, which now appeared to be a fortress with walls surrounding it.

The man steps outside the now fortress, wearing green and red pajamas, rubbing his eyes, indicating that he just woke up. He looks at the two and says, "My fellow crew said that I had company outside but couldn't believe it...look at the hour...I must admit you caught me off guard. I didn't even get a chance to freshen up."

Leonard and Elliott pay no interest but did notice the fortress set up on the shore with a dock now connecting the boat. The two don't ask where the materials came from to build such a thing because they lived by the philosophy that everything in the jungle was shared by all its inhabitants at least. They don't get distracted. They went there for business and are straightforward, down to the point, animals.

"We are interested in obtaining some of this Christmas, but what is it that you want in return?" Leonard asks while Elliott stands next to him in silence.

"I knew you couldn't resist the joy of Christmas. Nobody can, even if they try," the man says with a huge smile. "What I seek in return is gold. How much do you have?"

"Gold? I don't think we have any. All that we have is our duty to protect this jungle and the animals in it. We can offer you our favor if that's what you'd like," Elliott tells the man, confused at this concept of bartering and trading, which is still new to him.

"Ahh. Okay. Well, I'm not really interested in favors. What I will take in return for your requested amount of Christmas is land. I'm sure the gold will come later."

"Land? For you to keep? What will happen to those animals that are removed for your newly gained land?" Elliott asks, with a sense of worriedness.

"Well that's what they must forfeit to gain this Christmas. They have to figure that out for themselves," the man says with a frown and then asks, "Don't you believe in their ability to know what they want, to choose the wiser of two decisions?"

Leonard and Elliott, having heard enough, leave together to discuss what to do. Leonard, persuaded by the man's reasoning, now believes that the animals should be allowed to decide for themselves. Elliott, still unclear as to what action must be done, says little. So Leonard goes out to the riverbank and tells everybody the news that if they want Christmas then they must give the man their land in return.

It was finally the morning of the ceremonious summit. Leonard and Elliott, standing there wearing their finest twigs and leafs, are joined by their closest of kin on both sides of them. The seats are arranged in an oval. The decor is brown and green because all they had to use was leaves and dirt, and the summit overlooks the ocean horizon, and the sun is blocked by a thick cloudy sky.

"We welcome all of you," Elliott says in a commanding voice with his eyes shut and continues to say, "to discuss the coming holiday of--" Elliott immediately notices, as soon as his eyes open, that there's nobody in attendance. Leonard, his kin, and Elliott's kin, all stand there awkwardly staring at Elliott as he is baffled by the small turnout. There was one animal there, a small Lemur, wearing a red Santa Claus hat.

"What is that thing on your head?" Elliott asks, still appearing flustered and disappointed by the fact that no animals came to the summit.

"It's a Christmas hat. The man told me I would need it. So, I got it. So, I ran here because now that I have it, where do I go now that I have no more land?" the small Lemur explains.

Elliott astonished and appeared to be enraged even, rushes out of the summit and heads for the man's fortress. Leonard follows Elliott not knowing for sure what he has planned. As they make their way to the shore, they notice demolished sections of the jungle, smoke rising in the distance where the man's camp is, how cold the air is, and animals sitting along the shore holding onto many colorful wrapped boxes.

As the two arrive to the fortress, which had grown twice in size, the walls now are made of stone, and a larger dock was built that's holding more giant boats. You could see people loading and unloading crates from the boat. There were people with axes heading into the jungle and coming back with wood. There were huge lines of animals waiting outside the fortress ready to get a piece of this Christmas.

They wait outside the gate for the man. They wait outside for minutes that soon turned into hours. They wait for hours, which turned into a day. They wait for days, which soon turned into a week. The man never comes. The jungle is being torn down, the sun stops shining, and snow starts falling for the first time in the history of this jungle. A huge sign is built. It has the crest from the boat that the man originally came from, that claimed all this property as private, and there are arrows pointing you out.

Leonard, lord of the lions, and Elliott, the Arch Elephant, ask themselves what they could do with the little power they had to correct everything or bring it back to the way things were. There wasn't anything that could be done by the animals. The two decide to celebrate their Cornucopia event in their reserved sections the man had left for them.

Leonard and Elliott walk themselves out, without saying a word, of the now privately owned property. They part ways once they reach the place reserved for lions and the other one reserved for elephants. These places are rocky and cold. Snow covers every-thing, the flowers are dead, and the water is frozen.

The two sit in their own separate, yet similar, reserves quietly looking up at the sky and the falling snow. Other animals lie there too, mostly their close kin, some with their brightly colored wrapped gifts that nobody opened. Some animals are still joyous about the boxes, Christmas trees, and all its required knick-knacks, while there are the others with sadness in their eyes missing the jungle for what it once was.

You could hear the animals in the jungle, from all the separate reserves, begin singing the same tune. Their first winter and their first Christmas didn't get in the way of it. This year's tune is one of melancholy. The melody is only half as loud as it usually was but particularly beautiful. In this time of great change, there is a special sense of togetherness in the hymn. Leonard and Elliott both smile at the sky and don't mumble a single tune. The two only sit and appreciate the Cornucopia event for all its beauty and joy. The two sit and realize that the greatest joy, of all holidays, was to have each other.

About the Author

Born and raised in southern California, Hector Ramirez has always had an interest for science, history, and politics. He has always considered himself to be an optimist and an opportunist, so he has taken many doors to see where they lead him. He is very engaged in the political scene, managing (with the help of others) online networks of thousands to support their candidates of choice by organizing people and volunteering at fundraisers. He also has political experience in the Youth and Government program, which was the highlight of his adolescence life, where he learned about the United States' complex political system, had the opportunity to speak his thoughts to crowds of thousands, and was informed on the many turmoils affecting the world. He graduated from Summit High School in La Quinta, CA and is currently an Economics major at College of the Desert.

Edited by Dr. C. White-Elliott

Christmas Joy

Hazel Ramos

"How can I be substantial if I do not cast a shadow? I must have a dark side also if I am to be whole."
-C. G. Jung

*****

To my beloved son Troy E. Asplund.
May you find yourself when you are lost.
*****

In a lovely small town, full of luscious green parks, beautiful big homes, schools, and art statues, everyone was celebrating Christmas. The floors of the green parks were covered with a light blanket of snow. The red school roofs were white with frost; the art statues had icicles dangling from them. All the homes had big, fluffy white clouds of smoke coming from the chimneystacks, and the air smelled of pine and fresh baked cookies.

In town lived a charming little family named the Smileys. Mr. Smiley was a very happy cheerful man. He always wore a smile on his face. He was tall, his body was round, and he had a head of snow-white hair and a beard to match. Mrs. Smiley was short, thin, had long white hair flowing down her back, and always wore glasses and a smile on her face. The Smileys had a son named Nicolas. Nicolas was only five years old. He was a chubby little boy. He had shiny, golden hair and green twinkling eyes. Only, Nicolas wore an upside down smile on his face. Nicolas was sad.

Nicolas was missing his best friend in the whole wide world. His best friend was named Joy. Joy was a yellow puppy dog. She had a soft thick coat of fur, big floppy ears, a red tongue, and a big cold, wet nose. Nicolas wasn't the only sad one. Joy was also sad. She was lost. Joy missed Nicolas very much.

Earlier that day, Mr. Smiley was bringing in the family's Christmas tree when Joy ran between his legs and dashed out the door. Being the curious puppy she was, Joy couldn't wait to explore the new world outside her comfy home. Very soon after, the Smileys realized Joy was gone. Mr. and Mrs. Smiley and

Nicolas quickly grabbed their coats, locked up the house, and ran to the car. Inside the car, the family buckled their safety belts and started driving down the street in search of Joy.

They drove slowly past the other homes. Not minding the cold, they rolled the windows down and called out for Joy. They stopped five streets down at little Joseph's house. Little Joseph was Nicolas' friend from school.

"Have you seen my dog?" Nicolas asked.

"No, I'm so sorry, Nicolas. I haven't seen your dog," said Joseph.

Nicolas' green twinkling eyes became flooded with tears as he walked back, got inside the car, buckled his safety belt, and continued his search for Joy. Mr. Smiley drove past the parks, past the schools, past the big beautiful houses, and past the art statues, but Joy was nowhere to be found.

The Smiley family headed home. Once home, Nicolas dashed to his room and threw himself on his bed. Mr. and Mrs. Smiley quickly followed in after him. Mrs. Smiley comforted Nicolas. She rubbed his back softly and with a gentle voice whispered in his ear saying everything would be all right and Joy would return.

"We are also feeling very sad, Nicolas," said Mr. Smiley. "We miss Joy, too," he added. "When you are ready, please come join us in decorating the Christmas tree. We can't do it without you," said Mr. Smiley.

Mr. and Mrs. Smiley softly walked out of Nicolas' room, so he could be alone for a moment. A few minutes later, Nicolas rose out of his bed, wiped the tears from his eyes, walked out of his room, and joined his family to decorate the Christmas tree.

****

Meanwhile in town, Joy was on an adventure. She walked past the parks, past the schools, past the big beautiful houses, and past the art statues. Joy walked, and walked, and walked. Joy walked so far she didn't even realize she was now leaving town. Joy was about to walk into a different town, a dark and gloomy town.

The town had no parks. The schools were old and beaten down, and the houses were missing windows, had boarded up doors, with big creaky gates, and the only art was the writing on the walls. The air did not smell like pine and fresh baked cookies. Joy knew she was not close to home anymore. Joy knew she was lost.

Joy was frightened. All she could think about was her beautiful home that had her comfortable bed. She missed Nicolas and Mr. and Mrs. Smiley dearly. *Oh, how I wish I were home. If only I could get home, I promise I will never leave again,* thought Joy. Joy wasn't walking anymore; Joy was running. She wanted to find her way home quickly. She ran, and she ran, and she ran. Until she saw a young, thin woman that had long, flowing hair and a big warm smile on her face. The young woman was sitting on a curb reading a book. *I wonder if she can help me,* Joy thought.

With a sad and lonely expression on her face, Joy slowly walked up to the young woman's side. The young woman could feel a soft, thick coat of fur brushing on her arm. The young woman's smile grew even wider when she saw Joy. Joy didn't know it, but the young woman loved dogs. She loved them so much and helped them all the time. She helped them find food, shelter, and their families. The young woman looked at Joy and with a soft, friendly voice said, "Hello, little puppy. Are you lost?" Joy wagged her little puppy tail to say yes. "Well, you worry no more my little puppy friend. I will get you back home safely."

The young woman could see a red candy cane shaped dog tag hanging from Joy's white collar. The dog tag had Joy's name and home address on it. "Nice to meet you, Joy," said the young woman. "My name is Mary, and I know exactly where your home is located." Joy felt so excited. She could hardly wait to be able to see her family, the Smileys, again. Mary gently picked Joy up and held her snuggly against her as she started walking toward Joy's house. Joy felt safe again.

Mary walked, and walked, and walked. And soon, the air started to smell like pine and fresh baked cookies. Mary walked on the light blanket of snow that covered the park grass, she walked past the frost covered red rooftops of the school, she walked past many big beautiful houses, and she chipped an icicle off as she walked past an art statue. Finally, Mary walked to a big white house, covered lightly with fluffy snow. The house had a large window and behind that window was the biggest, tallest, most beautiful Christmas tree Mary had ever seen. It was covered in the most glorious decorations, brightest lights, and had a shiny gold star sitting at the top. Joy's tail was really wagging. Mary knew she had made it to the right house.

Just as Mary reached out to knock on the door, Nicolas opened the door. Without hesitation, Joy jumped out of Mary's arms and leaped into Nicolas' waiting arms. Nicolas and Joy both fell back and landed on the warm, soft carpet. Joy happily licked Nicolas' face. Nicolas rolled around happily on the carpet. Mr.

and Mrs. Smiley heard all the happiness and ran into the living room to greet Joy. The Smileys invited Mary inside their home. They all laughed, smiled and drank hot coco. And on this Christmas day, Nicolas got his smile back and found Joy again.

About Author

Hazel Ramos was born in Los Angeles, CA and raised in La Puente, CA. She is the proud parent of a very intelligent six-year-old boy. She currently is a student of Psychology. She is a Registered Veterinary Technician, licensed in the states of California and Washington. She is an animal welfare activist.

Edited by Dr. C. White-Elliott

The Piano Man's Christmas

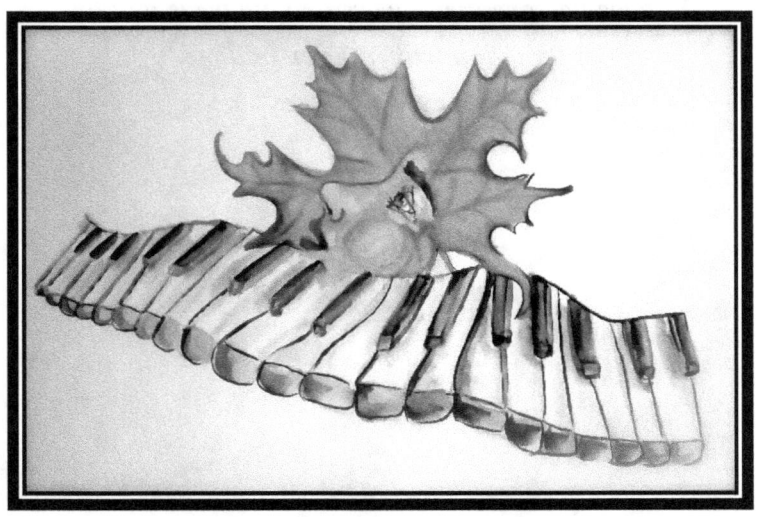

Janet M. Rumsey

"Can we become the flowers and the trees and live
as though it was just you and me."
-Janet M. Rumsey

One shaggy-haired man sat rehearsing in the tall window. The sound poured into the street warming the chill, a liquid melody greeting people on Olive Street. It was Christmas, and the streets were full of fallen red maple leaves.

Katherine, a girl of fifteen, darted out of 16 Olive Street. With her brow furrowed, she exhaled louder than the stroke of a piano key. Her long hair flew behind her like a cape. And a woman stood in the window looking out at Katherine, as she swung the wooden gate closed with a loud clap of the metal connecting.

She heard the piano man's melody, as soon as the thoughts about the argument with her mother dissipated. Why wouldn't her mother plan something else for Christmas? It was always the same. The crisp leaves crunched under Katherine's black boots as she walked downtown distracted by a familiar melody.

Katherine thought of the piano man as she continued along the street, wishing for a different Christmas tradition. She kicked the leaves for a simple delight, imagining it was her bare foot in warm sand. She approached an old woman, hair white as ivory piano keys and her scarf black and shimmery as the stool the piano man was perched on. The woman was holding a DVD player under her arm, the cord wrapped around it purposefully. Katherine matched strides with her, and they began to walk together.

"Did you get it fixed?" asked Katherine, trying to make conversation by gesturing softly to the silver box under the woman's arm.

Oh, no, the woman thought smiling. "I picked it up, so I could watch Christmas movies." She paused maneuvering a patch of grass in the sidewalk.

"Which is your favorite Christmas movie?"

"It's funny, you know, you never know when the next new technology is going to be invented. Tomorrow they might change the world!" She sang, ignoring the question.

Katherine laughed, "You're right. We never know until we know."

The woman stopped and looked at Katherine. "I always loved the movie *White Christmas*. I wanted the Mrs. Claus outfits that Rosemary Clooney and Vera-Ellen wore. To be wrapped in holiday red and sing until all the worries flew on by." She gracefully waved her left arm, her right still clutching the DVD player. "Oh, but you're much too young to remember that."

"I don't know that movie, but it sounds..."

"Oh, it was truly magical," she cut in. "Well, my dear. This is me," taking a step up the stairway to a house. The woman reached out her hand and squeezed Katherine's hand and smiled. Katherine squeezed and smiled back. "I always dreamed of a white Christmas because of that movie. I wish the trees were white and the streets dusted in sugar," she sang, walking up the red brick steps.

Katherine felt a sense of the Christmas spirit pulse through her. At times, she felt miserable enough that she wanted to be alone, and she had only felt that a short while ago. She found it entertaining that on a walk where she wished to be just with her thoughts, two people had affected her already. The piano man and the elderly woman entered her soul and changed her. A smile snuck across her face, and she again lunged for a brittle leaf.

She began walking back towards 16 Olive Street. As she rounded the corner, she could hear the piano man on the keys. She ducked under a naked tree branch and popped onto the street bouncing towards the music.

Katherine stepped closer and looked up at him in the big church window. She could hear the footsteps of his fingers flirt with the black and white keys. Over and over again, he moved repeating measure after measure. Soon, there was a silence, and he scratched the top of his head. He reached for his glasses on the side table, gently fixing them on his head. He leaned forward towards the piano and his large shoulders lifted up with a heavy inhale. He breathed in the last reminisce of the notes floating in the air and released.

His body quickly jolted and a pulse of energy darted through his body. He stood up, pushed in the stool and disappeared from her sight. She didn't think much of his departure, as a beautiful red poinsettia flower caught her eye in the garden next to the church. She picked one of the petals that had fallen to the ground and crossed the street again.

The door at her house stood taller than she had remembered. Maybe the world had made her smaller as the music consumed her. Maybe the old woman had squeezed her hand so hard that she shrank.

Or better yet, maybe she was a witch and made me shrink for being rude to my mother's Christmas tradition! Katherine thought looking down at the red petal. She spun it in her hand, like a pencil in the hand of an artist.

Her mind twisted and turned, but the petal kept her present. Its red color reminded her of the joy of Christmas and the beauty she had found on such a small adventure. As she opened the door, her family piano greeted her, but anger from the disagreement that morning burned within her still.

Maybe I'll just play, she thought as she set the petal on the dusty keys. It had wilted slightly, but was still vibrant.

The once forgotten notes jumped back into her head as she began to recall the smell of her piano teacher from long ago. She channeled the piano man in the church window and swayed her body as he did. She inhaled through her nose, and her fingers floated like falling petals on a dusty dinner table. Thoughts circulated in her mind as she began to push the familiar keys.

A car drove up the driveway, but Katherine didn't notice. The door opened and her mother stood in the doorway draped in red, ready for Christmas Eve dinner. She was a tall woman with wild hair. Katherine looked up and felt afraid, but her mother quickly came towards her.

Her mother placed a cold hand upon Katherine's back, and Katherine straightened her spine. Her eyes closed to hold in the tears that came suddenly from her mother's touch.

"Have you ever heard of the movie *White Christmas* from the 50s, I think?" Katherine responded tickling the piano keys. Katherine could feel her mother's excitement through her hand.

"Yes! I grew up with that movie. My dad would sing in hopes for a Christmas white with snow."

Katherine turned to her mom. "Next year, could we go somewhere warm for Christmas, maybe with white sand and the palm trees glistening? Why do we have to stay here with our family?"

"I know you wish to do something new and exciting, but Christmas is about keeping traditions and being with loved ones."

"I don't want to eat lamb and mint jelly," Katherine whined again, "and mashed potatoes and couscous with Aunt Nancy's spices every single year...It's so cold here, and I just want to see a California Christmas!"

"Oh, my love, Christmas is about being with our relatives and keeping up traditions. They love to see and talk to you. I would love to have you play the piano at Grandpa's house. Do you think you would want to do that tonight?" asked her mother playing with her long hair.

Katherine thought of the seasonal melodies in the street that she received from the old woman and the piano man. She nodded her head to answer her mother's question.

Katherine squeezed into her black and red dress, wriggled into her tights, and put on her satin shoes. She met her parents at the door. As they exited onto the street, Katherine noticed the absence of the piano's melody, but she began humming along with her mother singing, "I am dreaming of a white Christmas" from the old woman's favorite Christmas movie. As they descended the steps, Katherine smiled and crunched a leaf under her shoe.

"I love you more each day, my dear," sung her mother as they got into the cold car.

About the Author

Snoring snails, quacking cats, coughing coffee. Life is about looking at the world weirdly and then making art. Janet Rumsey is an artist from San Francisco, who has self-published children's books about environmental issues and is constantly coming up with new ideas with her preschoolers. She is looking to pursue a career in writing and creation. Janet believes inner peace comes from compassionate practice and children are the best link to the secrets nature has for us.

Edited by Dr. C. White-Elliott

Him for Her
and
Her for Him

Lee Saunders

"You know you are in love when you can't fall asleep because reality is finally better than your dreams."
-Dr. Seuss

Somewhere in the greater north of the Americas, where the sun rose between pinewoods and rested behind a mountain, a woman was asleep in her isolated cottage during the middle of the winter season. She awoke in bed, alone, as she usually does. She never did get used to him being at home in the morning. She doesn't spend the rest of the day missing him, but she does yearn for him to return back to her.

She starts the day by making the bed directly after getting out of it. She can still see the imprint of his body in the bed; she can see where he had laid the previous night. She loved the way he would lay next to her. He would nuzzle up to her with his back to the cracked window, which would allow a draft to come in and rest in the air. He would block the breeze from her just for her comfort. She stopped her daydreaming and flattened the bed and fluffed the pillows.

As she started picking up after her husband's attempt at putting his clothes in the hamper, it made her angry, but it also made her laugh at the fact that she married a man-child. Even when he was a firefighter, he was always goofy and enjoyed playing football with his buddies or having a Nerf gunfight with his fellow firefighters inside the station. She remembers walking in on them, dumb struck, during an all-out war in the middle of the garage where the engine should have been. She shook her head and proceeded to picking up the mess that was left behind by her husband.

She made her way through their tiny cottage to the laundry room. The washing machine and dryer are stacked on top of each other in a cabinet next to the spare fridge that her husband keeps the wine and beer they intend to drink. The room had a coat rack filled with jackets and heavy coats. There were boots on the floor by the back door, which led to the garage. There were only two boots on the threshold of their back entrance. They were all her husband's; one was a pair of work boots, and the others were more like galoshes. The snow and rain causes the land around them to get marsh-like.

She started sorting their clothes: colored and whites, delicates and regulars, regulars and heavies. She didn't exactly see this life in her future when she first met her husband. She was a first grade school teacher back before they moved out to where they are now.

She met her husband when she was teaching at the school she worked at. He was a brawny fireman who came for Fire Awareness Day at the school. All of the kids loved him because he was big and strong, the kind of man who a child would look at and say, "I want to be just like him when I grow up." He asked her to help him show the children how to carry someone in a fireman's lift, and he literally swept her off her feet and ran around with her over his shoulder.

The firemen gave their speech about fire awareness, and they were getting ready to leave when he went up to her and asked her if she would like him to come in on another day and talk to her class directly. She was flushed at the fact that this Greek god of a man had come over to talk to her. She never really was good with boys growing up, and she didn't get any better at it when she became an adult. She said, "Sure. That would be great." He came to her class a week later and presented with his gear on what fireman do and how they put out fires. When the class was dismissed for recess, she approached him.

"That was a great presentation," she said with a smile as he packed his gear away.

"Thank you," he said smiling back. "You have a great bunch of students."

"Yes," she replied a little discouraged. "They're all great..."

"Would you like to get some dinner?" he interrupted.

She was taken aback. "Um, well I…"

"Oh, I get it. You're already seeing someone," he said in a letdown voice. "It's okay. I understand."

He was flushed and looked embarrassed. He was rambling on, and she thought it was kind of cute. "Stop," she said with a smile. "I'm not seeing anyone, and I get off work at five." It was his turn to be dumb-struck; she handed him a piece of paper with her number on it, and she walked to the teacher's lounge to get coffee.

They went out to dinner later that week. This spawned the first date of their relationship. They continued to date for another few years until one night on the day of their third anniversary of being a couple, he got down on one knee and asked her to marry him. She said yes, and they were engaged for the next ten months. They had a small ceremony with only family and close friends. They didn't have many friends. All they needed was each other, *him for her and her for him.*

They continued their lives together for the next half a decade, doing the same pattern, going to work, going on date nights, vacations and other things that normal couples do. She decided that she wanted to have a child, so they tried, but they ran into some complications. They kept trying and failing, trying and failing. They were worried, so they went to see a doctor about it, and they hoped for the best, but they got the worst. She could never have children. That put their marriage on the rocks, but they managed to pull through with counseling. She grew depressed and distant and wasn't herself for a long time.

As most firefighters do, he retired early, for he had saved up a lot for their retirement. He wanted to move out of the city. He didn't much care for the hustle and bustle of the great metropolis they lived in, and she didn't much care for it either and was ready to settle down for good. They started looking for rural areas in the province, everywhere from cabins in the woods to farmhouses near small towns. They found a nice cottage up in the isolated area in the province they already lived in. They both seemed to like it, so they moved in.

They had been living in the cottage for over two years now, and they couldn't be happier. The cottage was located thirty minutes out of town, well, at least the forest was. Their home was located inside the forest. Their house was up a windy dirt road that was surrounded by the forest. It was in the middle of a clearing, a few minutes' drive from the start of the road. The house was made of wood, very old fashioned. It had a stone chimney rising from the right side of the house. The inside of the house was small and cozy. It had a living room with a fireplace and a kitchen with a wood stove. There was a laundry room in the back and a study on the other side of the house. It was a house to settle in, and that exactly what they were looking for.

They have been living in the cottage for two years now. She would stay home, and he would go out and collect firewood, go grocery shopping, hunt or look for things in the store to improve the house. She would clean around the house and cook dinner when he returned home with groceries.

She went back to folding the laundry. She had been going into these daydreams a lot recently. She was so bored in the cottage without her husband. He knew how to make the best of a boring situation. He would come up with some type of game or anything to pass the time.

The Christmas holidays are coming up, or they could have passed. She didn't know, for she had no access to a calendar. Christmas was her favorite holiday, but she had grown distant from it. She was sad; she was all grown up. She was retired, but could have no kids, and her husband was gone most of the day. She felt her depression flood back into her heart. She started to cry, and she dropped the laundry she was doing and ran back upstairs and threw herself on top of the finely lain sheets. She knew why she got upset, but she couldn't explain why it was impacting her that hard right then. She didn't know what to do with herself, so she just laid there.

"Hey, honey." She heard the bedroom door open. "Come downstairs. I want to show you something." It was her husband. She was too ashamed to see him; her eyes felt crusty with dried tears and her face was flushed, as it usually was when she cries. Her husband sat next to where she was laying on the bed.

"Come downstairs. I've got something to show you," he repeated. She sat up with dry tears across her face. He saw the tears and was taken aback for a moment, but his face went back into a smile.

"What is it?" she asked him with her bottom lip trembling.

"Come with me," he replied with a smile. He grabbed her hand and started leading her downstairs. As she followed him, she wondered why he was so cheery while she was so down. She was confused to the border of anger. She was about to question him, but they had reached the stairs. She saw a glow from the bottom of the stairs emanating from the living room.

Her hand was warm in his firm one as they took the last step down the stairs. Her jaw dropped when she turned into the living room. The whole room was covered in Christmas lights, and the fireplace had a warm blaze that licked the fresh logs that had been recently placed on it. There was a decorated tree placed to the left of the fireplace. It had been freshly cut from the forest surrounding their home. She looked around at it all and then at her husband in surprise.

"How did you…" she started.

"Shhhh," he cut in. "I want to enjoy this moment."

"What moment?" she asked him confusedly.

"This one, the one where you're smiling."

Her smile was about as radiant as the lights all around her. She couldn't believe what her husband had done for her. She looked at him and asked, "When and how did you do this?"

"Well," he started, "I know that Christmas was your favorite holiday back in the day, and I know we've failed to celebrate the annual tradition for the past few years, so I thought I'd make this one special just for you."

She could not stop looking at her husband. She fell in love with him all over again, and she started to remember why she loved him so much. He was all she wanted. He was her family, and he was her friend, the only one she ever needed. *Him for her and her for him.*

About the Author

Lee Saunders was born in 1997, in San Bernardino, CA. His family lived in Highland and then moved to Redlands when he was two years old. They put him in a private school where he had few chances to express any creative writing. He graduated high school in 2015 and started at Crafton Hills College that fall where he aims to be a firefighter.

Edited by Dr. C. White-Elliott

The Change on Mist Hill

Jessica Yslas

"I've lived what feels like a thousand years to feel your
kiss but my little mate, I'm in charge.
He said huskily, an air of authority lacing his words."
— K.A. Cross, Life on the Rocks

Diary

Day 1- The day it all started.

This is so new to me. I don't know what to do, so I am going to start the way I think it should start. My name is Emilie Dawn. I live in a small city called Raven City, with the population of two thousand two hundred and seventeen people. Even with its name, there is not a single raven that exists here in this little city of mine. Growing up in this city, people have always heard the rumors about the house on Blake Mist Hill. The tale that is told is about a family that lived there one hundred years ago that simply disappeared after living there for only five months. The family's disappearance is now known as the Lost Mist. After their disappearance, the hill was named after them. Actually, it was named after the youngest child. His name was Blake Mist.

In the five months that they had lived there, they had gotten so close to the town's people. They even helped the people in need. After the family's disappearance, the town's people decided every twenty-five years the town would hold a fake search and rescue three days before Christmas. At this event, they have a person place a trunk in the woods surrounding the house, and the person has to wait until midnight when the search and rescue is over. If someone finds the trunk this year, he/she will get to have a free dinner from the corner brick bistro.

There have been rumors that there is someone who can be seen roaming the house's property. People think it might be a ghost though that is highly unlikely because that would be crazy. Also, I would have seen my father by now if that were true. Well, yesterday was the day of the search and rescue, and I was chosen to be the one person to hide the trunk and oh so happily watch it until someone finds it. Whoopee for me. I had hoped for it to end fast. However, that is not what happened to me that night. Everything seemed to go in the opposite direction, and it has changed my life as I have known it to be up to now.

Emilie

December 22, 2020

I looked into the wood's tree line, and all I could see was darkness. I felt a shiver run down my spine, making all the hairs on my arms and neck stand up on ends. At the sensation, I started to feel as if someone were watching me from the woods. I started to feel scared, and I did not want to go in. I then turned around and faced my friend Christina Ballantine. "I don't want to do this any longer. Please don't let me do this," I pleaded with her.

"Don't you dare look at me with those puppy dog eyes. You know I can't stop this even if I am the mayor's daughter. You were chosen, and you seemed so excited about it. What happened? Why do you want to back out now?" Christina asked as she raised her eyebrow up in wonder.

"I just don't want to do it any longer. Come on. Look at the woods. They are creepy, and don't you get the feeling that you are being watched? I will do it only if you join me out there to keep me company," I said as another shiver ran down my spine. I looked back to Christina to see her look at me un-amused.

"Grow up. You wanted this, and you are going to get it because there is no way we can get a replacement at this time, so you are out of luck. I am sorry, but there is nothing I can do, and you know that I haven't liked the woods since I was little. I am sorry, but I just can't do it even if you are my best friend. I am truly sorry. See you when you get found okay," Christina stated as she handed me a flashlight and a map before starting to walk back to her midnight blue Ford F150.

She then climbed into her truck, started it up, and drove off, leaving me with nothing but the chest and a flashlight. I then quickly turned on the light and faced the woods, swallowing my fear and heading in. With the map in hand and the flashlight on, I started to head to the center of the woods to get to the spot I remembered I used to hide in when I used to play with my older brother Mark in the woods. That was until he passed away in an accident while walking home from school. Finally, I made it to a safe spot in the woods. I went to a giant tree next to the Mist house that has two hide-away cubbies, and I climbed into the bigger one. I put the box in the small one right below me that was behind some bushes. I then sat down and noticed that the tree faced towards the house.

As I sat there looking at the house, the moon was shining high in the sky. The house is a three-story building with lots of windows. I noticed movement inside the house on the third floor. What I saw looked like a person, so I started to get a bit closer to get a better look. That was when I saw movement again. That time I could make out what it was, and to my surprise, it *was* a person, and it looked as if the person was looking at me though he/she probably could not see me. Then, I heard a sound to my right, and I quickly ducked back into my hiding spot, as a light went over a tree in front of me. That was when I heard people talking.

"Hey, David, where do you think the hider is?" asked the man.

"I don't know, but I heard that the hider is a girl this time. How much do you bet that she hid the chest and went home not wanting to stay out here? I even heard that there is something valuable in the chest and that is the only reason we are out here," stated David.

When they were speaking, I suddenly got the feeling that they were not good people and that I should not show myself to them for some odd reason. They then started to walk away. That was when I heard a very loud howl that sounded close by. It frightened me because it sounded as if it was right behind the tree I was in.

"Dude, you heard that right?" said David.

"Yeah... let's get out of here. I don't want to be here when that thing shows up," stated the other man with a quivering voice.

I then heard the sound of running footsteps going away from me in what sounded like the direction they had come from. All I could think was, *What the heck was that?* and that was when I heard the sound of something running. It sounded as if were coming up to me, but I saw it pass by. The creature was big... it sort of looked like a wolf but a lot larger. As I was thinking, the creature stopped, and I swear it was looking at me. I could not help but to stare at its blue eyes that seemed to glow. As I looked it in the eyes, I felt the urge to get closer, but my body would not let me. I could feel the animal looking at me before it turned and headed in the direction that the men had just gone in. As I watched it leave, I noticed I did not feel fear from seeing the creature. I sat there waiting for seven minutes to see if anybody screamed because I thought the giant wolf was going to attack someone that was on the search.

Looking at my watch, I realized it was five minutes until the search was considered over and everyone had to stop looking for the chest. That was when I took out my cell phone only to notice that my battery was dying and the alarm I had set was about to go off in three minutes. Right before my phone died, my alarm went off signaling that the search was over and that I could go home. As I was climbing out of the tree very slowly in case the giant wolf came back, my left foot got caught in the small cubbyhole. I fell and landed on my back, just as my foot came out of the hole.

When I went to get up, I could not help but to cringe because as I took a step onto my left foot, pain shot up my leg. I was so preoccupied with the pain that I did not see a man come up behind me until he coughed to let me know he was there. Due to his sudden appearance, I jumped slightly in shock. I could not help myself when I found myself staring at him. I quickly turned my head away to hide my blush. When I looked back at him, I saw as small smirk on his face and his light blue eyes shimmered with a sort of joy that you see in a child's eyes when he is pure.

After I found myself looking into his eyes, I remembered the chest. So, I quickly turned back to the tree to retrieve it. As I was pulling the chest out, he spoke, "What are you doing out here?" I could tell that he really did not care by the tone of his voice. *He has a sexy voice,* was all I could think, as he spoke.

"Um... getting myself hurt," I said back with the same tone of voice. "Oh and trying to be oh so happy that I have to walk to the edge of the woods, so I can get picked up. Oooo maybe I'm trying to give myself hypothermia...that sounds like a lot of fun," I said as I hobbled away in the direction I had come from in annoyance.

"You know there are some wild animals out here, and that it is dangerous at night," he said in a much softer tone. That was when I turned around to look him in the face to tell him off.

"I did not want to be out here for your information... when I was chosen to be the hider, I was happy, but when I got here today, I got the feeling that I should not be out here at all... I was unable to back out, so here I am," I stated with a huff, while blowing my hair out of my face. I then started to turn around; as I did so, I thought I saw his eyes glow a bright blue, so I quickly turned my head to face him and saw that his eyes were normal, which set my nerves on high for some reason and made my body start to shake.

Then, I noticed the moon was about to be covered by the clouds. So, I took my eyes off the strange man for a split second. But when I looked back in his direction, I saw he was no longer there. For some reason, that scared me, so I turned around and started to walk back to the wood's edge. As I stumbled through the woods getting scraped and cut by bushes and tree branches on my arms and face, I heard the sound of leaves moving behind me. I started to hobble faster to get to the clearing as the noise got closer to me. Suddenly, I heard it: the sound of a wolf howling and something behind me lurking - probably waiting for me to fall.

With that thought in my mind, I turned around to face it. But, because I am so smart, I wanted to keep walking. So, walking backwards I ended up hitting my head on something very hard. At that exact moment when my head collided with the hard object, my vision started to go black as an object jumped at me from the bushes. All I felt before my vision went black was excruciating pain.

I woke to find myself in a room lying on a king-sized bed with midnight blue sheets. As I noticed that I was actually in the bed itself, it hit me like a stone, and I thought, *Am I still wearing my clothes...Oh God, please don't let me be naked.* As I pulled the blanket off my body slightly, I could see that I was still wearing my clothes. I let out a sigh of relief. After I did that, I thought, *It is time to get out of here.*

When I got off the bed, I noticed the room was very nice. It had a Victorian feel to it. The walls were painted a light brown with a white trim across the top and bottoms of the walls. There was a door that was slightly ajar, and inside there was a flickering light. As I went to open the door, I noticed my arm was bandaged up, and it looked as if blood was seeping through. All I could think was, *I will take care of it later.* I then pulled the door open only to find out that beyond the door was a candle lit hallway. I then cautiously stepped into the hallway and looked to the right and saw a light blue light. To the left side of the hallway, all I could see was darkness.

I turned in the direction of the light and away from the darkness and slowly made my way down the hall until I reached a staircase that went down. I then slowly descended the stairs being careful to not make any noise. As I got to the last three steps, I stopped in my tracks to see if anyone was down there, and when I saw no one, I decided that the coast was clear. When my foot left the last step, I quickly headed in the direction of what looked to be a door next to a window.

"I would not do that if I were you." At the sound of that voice, I could not help but to jump out of fear, and that was when the adrenalin kicked in. I quickly spun around only to not see anyone there. All I could think was, *I must be hearing things...Great, I have gone nuts.* I then turned back to the door only to hear the voice say, "Are you stupid? I told you not to do that." Then, I turned around, I stood there trying to see if I could see someone in the dark room. That was when I saw him- the person who had just spoken, though I could only slightly see his outline. When the person stepped forward, I saw that it was the man from before I blacked out: the one that had me drooling over him.

"Why should I stay... are you going to hurt me if I do it again?" I asked as I looked at him in annoyance.

"If you go out there, they are going to kill you," he stated as he leaned against the fireplace. At that statement, my whole body froze as my eyes widened.

"What the hell are you saying...are you threatening me? How dare you...you have no right to threaten me like that. I don't even know you, and you think you can keep me here...stop kidding yourself," I stated as I turned and grabbed the handle and pulled the door open. When I did that, I suddenly felt his presence right behind me, as he ripped the door from my hand.

He then whispered in my ear and said, "Do you see the man out there with a gun? He is here to kill you." After he said that, I looked in front of me, and I didn't see anyone. Then, all of a sudden, my eyesight increased, to let me see a man facing my direction with a gun. He started to raise it in my direction as if getting ready for fire. That was when I saw a spark of fire and felt an arm go around my waist and pull me off to the side of the door facing a chest. Fear struck deep into my core. I then started to shake as I brought my hands up to the chest in front of me. As I did so, I realized who it was in front of me, and I could not help to think about how hard his chest was and how I was there right then. As I turned away from his chest, I saw that the sofa had a hole in it.

He leaned into me and whispered in my ear, "That is why you can't leave."

"Why... is this happening to me... why does he want to kill me?" I said as tears started to stream down my face as I shook.

"You are being hunted. I am too but for another reason," he stated as held me close.

"Why me though?" I asked while I looked up to his face, as I slightly pulled on the front of his shirt.

"You were bitten in the woods," he sadly stated as he lifted my arm in front of my face.

"By what and why would that make it so I am being hunted by people the day after I was bitten?" I asked in concern.

"Well...it was a werewolf, and well, it has not been only one day. You have been out for about a week, and this werewolf is no ordinary werewolf...it is a very rare type of werewolf," he responded to my question.

"What makes this werewolf so rare... that I would be hunted because of it?" I asked as I took a step back to get a better look at him as he responded because I had a gut feeling he was not telling me something and that something might be very important information that I needed.

"This werewolf is an alpha and can change any time he wants to change, and there is a legend that he is immortal and that whoever he bites will become his mate and will live for all eternity with him," he replied, as he looked me in the eyes. As he spoke, it felt as if he was talking about himself or someone he knew.

"Really, who is this werewolf that bit me since you happen to know that it was a male?" I asked as I placed my hands on my hips and stood with my feet slightly apart and leaned on my right leg as I faced him. Though at the time all that was going through my head was, *It was him. He did this to me.* And yet, I had no clue as to why I was thinking that, but it felt just right.

"I am truly sorry... but it was an accident." As he spoke, there was a look of sadness in his eyes that said he was truly regretful. That was when it hit me... it really was he who bit me, and I could not help but to take a step back out of shock and strangely it was not out of fear that he is a werewolf. That somehow settled very well with me. As I did that, I saw him see the realization in my eyes as to who it was by seeing the sadness pass through his eyes.

"I am truly sorry. I was just trying to catch you before you fell and hit your head again. I thought I would be able to hold you without drawing blood or turning you in any way, but the two men from before when you were in the tree came out of nowhere, and it shocked me because they had guns with them, and they took aim to fire at me with you next to me, and my jaw just tightened on its own. I only realized I had drawn blood when I tasted it as I let go to scare them away and to prevent them from shooting in your direction." He was sad as a solemn look passed over his features.

"Oh!" That was all I could say when I heard his reasoning. "I don't know what to say other than thank you for saving me from getting shot. But for some odd reason, I understand how it was a mistake and how you did not mean to bite me... I do not know why I do, but I do. So, don't blame yourself. Plus, I was not thinking when I started to walk backwards. I was just scared from all the sounds I was hearing, which I am guessing was you from the start which also explains why when I first saw you in human form, your eyes glowed electric blue," I said with a slight smirk on my face.

He then drew closer to me, and I could not help but feel calmer as he got closer to me with each step until he was right in front of me as he placed his hands on my hips after removing my own hands from my hips.

"So what do we do now that I am being hunted along with you as well?" I asked as I placed my hands on his chest, which seemed natural as I looked into his eyes.

All he said next was, "Well, I guess we get to know each other while we are on the run."

"Well then, may I know what your name is first before we start our getaway?" I asked in a sultry manner.

"Oh, my name...well, I guess that would be a good start. Wouldn't it? Well, my name is Blake Mist, and yes, I am the one that this hill is named after, and yes, I am a part of the original Mist family, and I am considered the last living member of that family." As he said that, I could not stop my mouth from falling open in shock and awe. "The rest of my family has been hunted down and killed. So, there is my name and back story. Now, may I know your name?" he asked, as he slowly got closer to my face.

I responded by saying, "My name is Emilie Dawn. I was born and raised here in Raven City all my life. I have no family. My parents died two years ago, and I just graduated last year from high school. So, now you know practically everything about me. Now what do we do next?"

"We run away from here together because they saw me with you, which means we don't stop until we are safe and sound in a place we can call home permanently," he whispered in my ear and then pulled back and pressed his warm lips to mine, which signaled the start of our adventure together, and somehow all of that felt just right to me- like that was my destiny.

About the Author

Jessica Yslas is a young woman who was born and raised in La Quinta, California. She has been published once before by CLF Publishing, LLC. She loves to read supernatural romances, which inspire her to write her own stories that were supernatural romances. She will be continuing her previous story from *The Love Mosaic* called "Interlaced" in *The Love Mosaic II* that will be released next year.

About the Editor

Dr. Cassundra White-Elliott resides in California with her family, where as an English/Education professor she teaches at various community colleges and universities.

When writing, she writes with the direction of the Holy Spirit, in an effort to share with God's people all that He has for them.

In addition to teaching and writing, Dr. White-Elliott also serves as an evangelistic teacher. She is the founder of International Women's Commission, a ministry that serves the needs of the entire person, by attending to healing the mind, body, soul, and spirit.

Dr. White-Elliott holds a Ph.D. in Education, a Master's in English Composition, and a Bachelor's in Education.

Dr. White-Elliott is also the founder of CLF Publishing, LLC. For publishing, go online to www.clfpublishing.org.

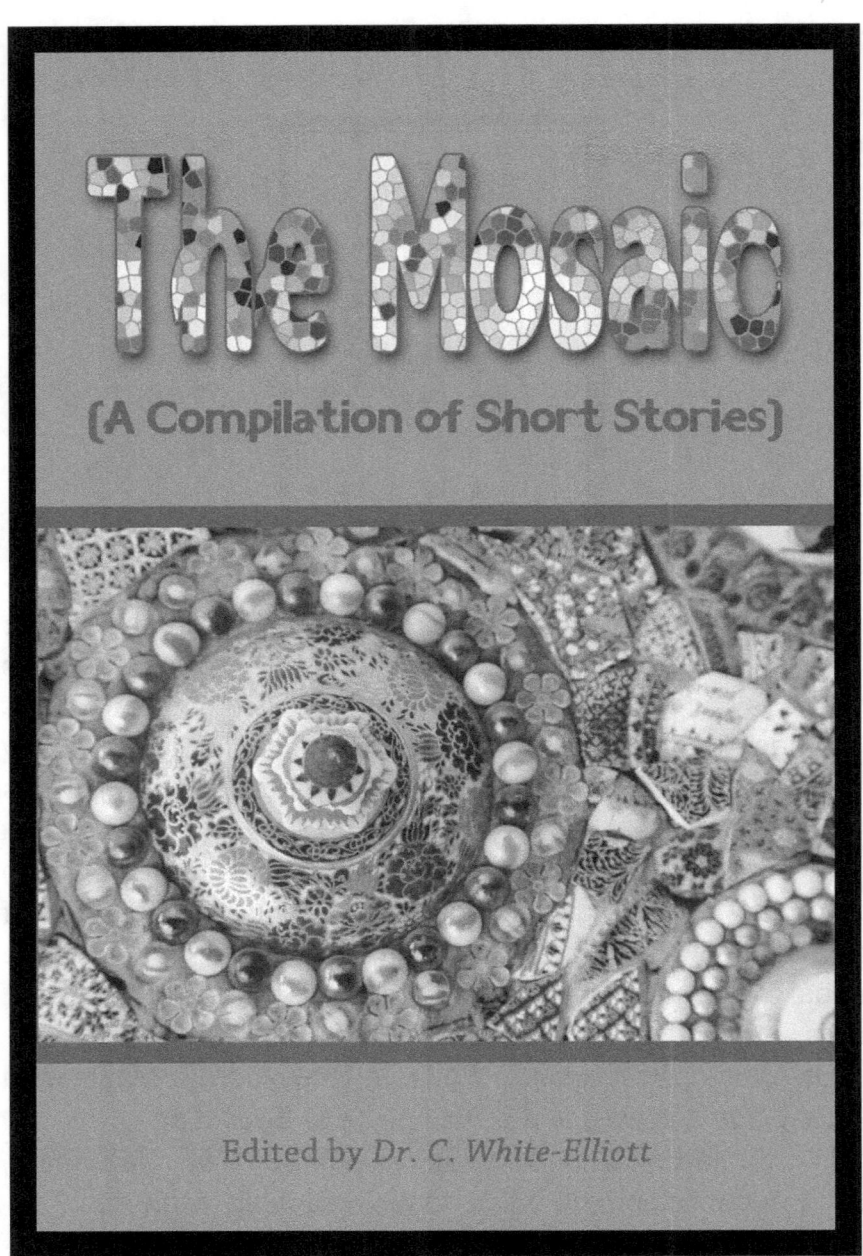

Get your copy of the first "Mosaic" at barnesandnoble.com or amazon.com.

The Mosaic
(A Compilation of Short Stories)

The Mosaic is a collection of fourteen short stories written by fourteen different authors who wonderfully display their talent and their unique expression of creativity. The genres range from science fiction, to action, to suspense, to adventure, to fantasy, to drama.

Featured in this compilation are the following authors: Celine Acuna, Marissa Davisson, Kimberly Enriquez, Raena Fisk, Sandra Flores, Caroline Foster, Alexander Francisco, Mariah Halbert, Mone Makkawi, Stacey Ogden, Zak O'Mara, Jason Quezada, Kayghee Reynolds, and Gary Rodriguez.

sci-fi adventure action
fantasy drama fantasy suspense
eroticism action drama
suspense action eroticism
adventure action sci-fi suspense

CLF Publishing, LLC.
www.clfpublishing.org

www.creativemindsbookstore.com
www.amazon.com
www.barnesandnoble.com

ISBN 978-0-9960815-5-9
90000

9 780996 081559

It is a wonderful collection of short stories from a variety of genres.

Edited by *Dr. C. White-Elliott*

Love is universal and quite mysterious. It comes when you least expect it- like a thief in the night. It can bring joy, and it can bring pain. Love can have you one day up but the next day down; love can have you turning like a merry-go-round. Love goes where the heart takes it.

Love can be communicated and understood by a simple touch, a look, a kiss, or a hug. It can be communicated through a song, a poem, in a greeting card, and even through a love story. The story may have a happy ending- if all goes well. But that, of course, is not guaranteed. Before you know it, something can go unexpectedly wrong!

This compilation of love stories will have you on the edge of your seat. Some may bring joy to your heart, while others will cause you to shed a tear.

Each story shares love from a different vantage point. Some display love erotically, while others exhibit platonic love.

The stories included within this book bring love right to you in a manner you have never seen.

Featured in this compilation are the following authors: Katie Abbott, Samantha Blackwell, Michael Bril, Megan Duarte, Clarissa Flowers, Yadira Fuentes, Gavin Keays, Karen Lopez, Stacey Ogden, Zak O'Mara, Danyelle Pappas, Kayghee Reynolds, Meagen Sais, Daisy Sekly, Alexandria Stapleton, Haylee Vaughan, Jessica Yslas.

Eroticism *Platonic*
Nature *Family* Animals Mystery
Unthinkable
Suspense Travel

CLF Publishing, LLC.
www.clfpublishing.org

www.creativemindsbookstore.com
www.amazon.com
www.barnesandnoble.com

ISBN 978-0-9961971-0-6

90000

9 780996 197106

The Mosaic II

Edited by *Dr. C. White-Elliott*

Take an adventure within the pages of **The Mosaic II**, where you will find stories filled with controversy, intrigue, mystery, amazement, and inspiration.

This compilation features the following authors: Samantha Blackwell, Tayani R. Davis, Kimberly Enriquez, Kathleen Hallo, Andy Halsig, Zak O'Mara, and Gary Rodriguez.

Eroticism *Platonic*
Nature *Family* Animals Mystery
Unthinkable
Suspense Travel

CLF Publishing, LLC.
www.clfpublishing.org

www.creativemindsbookstore.com
www.amazon.com
www.barnesandnoble.com

ISBN 978-0-9961971-2-0
90000

9 780996 197120

www.ingramcontent.com/pod-product-compliance
Lightning Source LLC
Chambersburg PA
CBHW051143020726
47501CB00005B/1648